Little **BUFFALO** River

Frances Beaulieu

McGilligan Books

Canadian Cataloguing in Publication Data

Beaulieu, Frances
  Little Buffalo River

ISBN 1-894692-00-4

1.Métis — Northwest Territories — Fiction. I. Title.

PS8553.E2239L57 2000   C813'.6   COO-932246-9
PR9199.3.B3765L57 2000

Copyright © Frances Beaulieu 2000

Editor: Sharron Proulx-Turner
Copy editor: Noreen Shanahan
Layout: Heather Guylar
Cover Design: Heather Guylar
Author Photo: Linas Brazyz
Map on page 159 adapted from the book *Denendeh* published by the Dene Nation.
All rights reserved. No part of this book may be reproduced in any manner whatsoever without written permission, except in the case of brief quotations in critical articles or reviews. For information contact McGilligan Books, P.O. Box 16024, 859 Dundas Street West, Toronto, ON, Canada, M6J 1W0, ph (416)538-0945, e-mail mcgilbks@idirect.com.

We acknowledge the support of the Canada Council for the Arts for our publishing program.

The Canada Council | Le Conseil des Arts
for the Arts | du Canada

Acknowledgments

Little Buffalo River is dedicated to the memory of my Ama, Victoire Alphonse, and to the memory of my mother, Nancy Morrison.

Marsi cho (thank you) to the following people; Ann Decter, Lillian Allen, John Grube and Sharron Proulx-Turner for teaching me and believing in what I wrote.

Marsi cho to Linas Brazyz, Kether MacDonald, Florence Laferty, Marion Kane, Phil Urbanski, Cate Stoker, Sue Walliser, the memory of Hugh Wylie, Dr. Robin Brooks-hill, and my cousin, Frances Beaulieu, for listening so well while I searched for my words through the years.

Marsi cho to my brothers and sisters for being, for surviving, and for growing.

And marsi cho to my granddaughters, Emma and Julie MacDonald for teaching me how to laugh and fly all over again.

Stories

Little Buffalo River 7

Fire and Tea and History 13

Whitehorse, by the light of the silvery moon 25

White Gloves and Pointed Shoes 37

Arsenic 43

Christmas Party 49

T'Atiste 65

Let's Pretend 73

Mommy Suzanne 81

Broom Story 97

The Devil's Work 105

Lemon Tree 111

Caribou Queen 121

Leaving Home 137

High Hopes 153

Little **BUFFALO** River

Flying high above the endless deepless sun-gleamed silk
of grey green water.
Great Slave Lake. Great Bear Lake. Rat River.
Close your eyes now
okay?

You are on a twin engine plane.
It's very small and noisy
a tan nylon strap holds you to a fuzzy red seat
with paper over the headrest and a faint smell of sick.

Precambrian rocks. Ponds. Little lakes. Liquid silver rivers flow far below.
The seats vibrate as the plane buzzes through clouds and icy blue air.
Then
you all float down from the sky
together in the metal bird
shivering. Riding the winds over pine treetops.
The bump of earth as you land.
The door opens
A warm breeze kisses both your cheeks in welcome
as you watch your feet
climbing down the little tin steps
from the plane
and you feel that everything can't help but be fine now.

There is a smell of sweet grass and wood smoke in the air.
You leave the plane and walk across the soft tarred runway
into the new.
Green grass electric blue blazing rose
cherry red wowzam pink
under the shaded umbrella trees at the edge of the tarmac.
Porcupine quills, fish scales, stained glass
with berry juice, iridescent flowers sewn
on brown velvet moose and caribou skin jackets and moccasins.

"Oh praise the Lord, thank God we made it. This is my home. Here. In Deninu. Yes, this is where I grew up in that damned convent," said Ama, brushing off her good navy blue skirt and smoothing her brand new flowered kerchief before leading the three children

over to meet the relatives.
Then the smiles and hugs and handshakes
the kisses on both cheeks
in the green grass.

The hot machine smell of oily smoke
shimmers as the silver airplane fades away in the flying sky clouds.
The aunties and uncles and cousins waving turquoise and lime
and popsicle pink coloured scarves
Waving shawls and lazy birch switches.
Goodbye
Goodbye to the plane.

Chamomile. Golden buds in the grass, sandy roads with smooth pebbles, one-room log cabins, canvas teepees to smoke fish, weasel houses.

"Nah," said an old auntie. "Those are no weasel houses, those are mink dens. A long, long time ago, when I was just a little girl like you…Oh! That was such a long time ago!" And everyone laughed. "There were French brothers here then, from Quebec. They wanted to make some stumpah, some money, for their mission here, eh? So, they built those little mink dens to raise mink and sell the fur. They didn't know how to go out on the trap line like everybody else. Hmmph. Anyways, it didn't work. The mink, they all died by the second winter. Maybe they didn't like those little houses the brothers made for them!"

Anna and Violette, little Harry and Ama, and all the aunties, uncles, and cousins thumped along the silvery wooden boardwalk through the sea-green mist floating above the shore. They carried the duffel bags and shiny metal blue suitcase across town to the little wooden house on the edge of the field where the mink dens slept in the golden waist-high grass.

"This is where we'll stay for the summer," said Ama and she boiled some tea, an old auntie unwrapped some warm bannock from a tea towel, and the uncle cooked some fresh whitefish outside, over the fire.

After, someone spread a big blanket under the spring lace of birch trees. Ama and the aunties sat, heavy brown stockinged legs straight out in front of them, kerchiefs pulled down around their necks. They passed the chewing tobacco and cigarettes and refilled their tea mugs. It was very warm. Harry fell flushed cheeks asleep on Ama's lap. Baby rain beads of sweat on his nose. Fat blue flies buzzed low and heavy over the empty enamel plates. The drone of crickets rose and fell forever under the sun.

Anna and Violette lay on their stomachs near the edge of the blanket, listening to Ama. She was telling them about the Little Buffalo River where they would be going by boat the next day.

"I'll take you to the house where I was born. Where I lived with my mama and papa and little brother.

"Maybe I was around five or six, I can't remember too good now. But the white man came to this part of the north, and they brought a sickness. My family all got sick. First my papa, then my mama and little brother. They all died one by one and I had to come here, into the town and live with the French nuns in the convent. But before that when I was just a little girl, like you and Violette, oh, I was so happy living on the Little Buffalo River."

Anna rolled over, closer to Ama's leg. "Why do they call it that, Ama?"

"Because a long time, oh many, many years before the whites

and the mission came, and even for a little while after, there were salt banks there by the water."

"Ama? Salt? Real salt? Like what we put on meat?"

"Real salt, my girls. It looked just like snow, there was so much...yes, piled up like snow banks, salt banks all along the little river. On both sides, as far as you could see. And sometimes in the evening as the sun was setting in the summer, my own mama, she would wave to my little brother and me

shhhhhh

she would whisper just so we could hear and we would come so quiet. We would sit down in the grass and we would watch. Then all along the banks the buffalo would come to lick the salt. Just like candy. Oh it was a big treat I tell you, for them to lick that salt. Hey-heyyy, my heart."

"Ama. You're crying, Ama?"

"No, it's all right, my girl...Well. The salt banks are gone now, Anna. No more buffalo in these parts. Still. The Little Buffalo River they call it. Yes. I was born here, where the buffalo were, and the salt. That goddamned white man."

"Ama?"

"Yes, my girl?"

"I'm part white, eh?"

"Yes, my girl."

Fire and Tea and **HISTORY**

Underneath the table was all hers. Anna's place…with oilcloth walls hanging down on all four sides. With lemon coloured pears, and blue grapes, and fat red tomatoes in little green-lined squares. A soft sleepy winter light shone through the rainbow fruit. Beneath the walls she could watch the glow of fire from the wood stove.

    She crouched on sleeping bags, smelling summer memories. Smelling warm sun canvas and wood smoke; high bush cranberries and drying fish and sweet grass. Finding little lost summer leaves in the folds. She was listening to the teacups scrape across her oilcloth roof.

Black Marie was visiting Ama. "Hey-eyy-yayy! My God my God...what's that thing under me? Anna! Aiii-eeeee Adelle, take a look under here, eh?"

Ama lifted the corner of the oilcloth and peered under the table at Anna, who was trying to make herself small behind the sleeping bag. She heaved her big sigh. "Ohhh. This one...tsk. And under the table again too eh? Always right under my feet, this Anna. Staring at the fire, too!"

Black Marie drummed her fat thunder fingers on Anna's roof. "Hey, you stop staring at the fire now — you'll pee-pee your bed tonight."

Ama thumped the teapot. "That's the devil's work for sure, looking in the fire like that. You stop now."

Black Marie began to giggle. "That big bogeyman, he'll *jump* right out an take you in the fire with him!"

"I'm telling you Marie...this little one. She has the devil's blood, full of no good, just like her mother!"

Underneath the table, Anna's heart lurched. She scrunched her knees up to her chest and held them tight. There was a rustling from above and then Black Marie's hand slid under the edge of the oilcloth, waving back and forth. Anna unfolded. She took the comforting stick of Double mint gum and the hand disappeared.

"Heyy. So. Where's that Suzanne now, Adelle? You got any news about her?"

Ama's chair scraped and a teacup cracked sharp on the roof.

"Hmmph! Who knows where that one is. You think that Suzanne lets me know anything? Even though I raised her like my own daughter? Even though I treated her like my own blood? No-siree. Nothing. Not a word from her. Suzanne is so haywire now, she brings nothing but heartaches to me. Anyways, she never was a mother to this poor little thing sitting under the table. I'm the one that scraped the shit out of Anna's little diapers when no one else would take her.

"You remember that time eh, Marie? Suzanne, she was trying to give baby Anna to anybody back then, even trying to give her away in the bar. Who can imagine such a thing! Then next thing I heard Suzanne, she's on her way to Edmonton with the other two kids and poor little baby Anna wound up with those no-goods that live down close to the bridge. What was in Suzanne's head? Giving a newborn baby away to a family of six boys, and not a crumb of food in the place for those kids. I hear that the mother was always drinking in the Ol' Stope or playing cards when her husband was out in the bush trapping.

"But that woman, she wanted a little girl so Suzanne gives her the baby right out of the hospital! She was so haywire with the booze then who knows what was going through her head? But what kind of a life was that for a new baby?

"A good thing I heard just in time and I went right over there and took Anna home with me. She was in a dirty swing crying her heart out! Her diaper's soaking wet I tell you! Yup…she's a little orphan, alright.

"Oh, but my heart aches when I think of that Suzanne though. I took care of Suzanne too, you know that, eh? I took her when her mother Bertha died in childbirth and all the little ones were left behind. Ernest, he was always out prospecting in the bush then, just in town for a few days here and there to load up and away he goes again, looking for his big dream, his big gold mine. His big pie in the sky. So what did he do then when his wife died like that all of a sudden? What does a man like him know about raising kids on his own? He could have got married again, but no, he had no time to look for a wife. No time to find a mother for those little orphans. He had to get rid of them all so he could go looking for that gold. Yes, and look at him nowadays, old and living all by himself in that house down by the Rex Café. Where's all his money now, eh? What good does it do him?

"Life is hard, eh, Marie? Yes, that was my old friend from when I was young...poor, poor Bertha, she left four little orphan girls behind her when she went to the grave. Suzanne was the youngest, then next was Doreen. Evelyn, she was the oldest girl.

"That old Ernest, he sent Doreen and Evelyn to Fort Smith to live with the nuns right away. I packed the bags myself and they were gone on the next plane, just like that. Poor little innocents, they didn't know what was going on at all, too young, just babies themselves. Ernest didn't want them to see Bertha, he didn't want them to see the burial." Ama sighed. A thick cloud of silence muffled Anna's little house.

After a few seconds, Black Marie scuffled her moccasins back and forth on the linoleum. A streaming golden arrow of chewing tobacco snapped dead centre into the spittoon across the room. Black Marie was very impatient, she didn't like to wait too long in the middle of a story.

Ama sighed again. "They say Doreen, she got polio right away in that residential school with the nuns. They sent her outside to Edmonton and no one ever heard another word about her, maybe she's dead by now."

"Too bad!" said Black Marie. "How about the other one? Evelyn. I hear she turned out real good, eh?"

"Oh yes," said Ama. "She married that nice Irishman, a real steady worker. They live up in new town with all their kids. Three boys, and three girls now, I hear. If only Suzanne turned out like her. Heyy.

"But the baby Bertha died from, they called that one Rose Marie. The nuns wouldn't take her, she was too young. Ernest, he just let that baby go. He sent her outside to live with some whites. He never said another word about it and nobody knows where she is now.

"Yes, I'm the one that took Suzanne then, when her mother died and the family was split up. She was only two years old, and I raised her like she was my own daughter. That's two generations I'm taking care of now, first Suzanne, now Anna…and what thanks do I get? Nothing. I did my best for that Suzanne I tell you and she treats me just like dirt. Nothing but men an' drink, men an' drink for her ever since her Louie was shot to death that one time in the fall when he went hunting. Nothing but men an' drink for her now, I tell you.

"That Louie…he was a good husband for Suzanne. I still remember like it was yesterday. He was so good-looking. He was going hunting, eh? They came to visit and he was saying to me I'm going to bring you a big moose for the winter, Adelle! No one will go hungry this year!

"Such a big smile he had…To think he pulled through the war without a scratch. He had a parachute, eh? He brought it back with him and I still keep it in the warehouse. Yes, he made it through that whole war, then he went hunting and *bang*, that's it for him. And a little while later, this little one came into the world without a father…and a mother gone straight to the devil…No, Suzanne's no mother. I'm the mother now to this poor little one…me! My God, my God, why me?"

Anna sat still and silent underneath the teacups and bannock.

In her little devil house. Picking her little devil nose. Her mouth full of sweet devil gum. Listening hard.

Marie packed away her chewing tobacco in one of her many pockets and took out her pipe. She lit it up and sighed. "Aiii-eee, it's a hard, hard life that God has given us, eh Adelle?"

"Hey...my friend, I'm telling you...that white man's God. He sure has funny ways sometime. Taking my Mama and Papa from me too, when I was so young. So long ago now. My little brother."

Ama sighed and sighed. She pushed her chair from the table. Anna watched her moccasins glide over to the stove. Ama brought the steaming tea kettle back and poured more hot water into the old brown teapot. Anna could hear the plonk of sugar cubes. She listened to the spoons clinking in the fresh cups of tea, stirring in the canned evaporated milk. Ama started talking again.

"My little brother, he was so fat and so sweet. I remember one time in the morning, we were fighting to see who would get the tin from the butter so we could lick it. Oh, he was a strong one, a husky baby, *strong* I'm telling you. He was pulling on one side, and me, I was pulling, pulling with all my might on the other edge. We were so stubborn! And greedy too, we both wanted to lick that tin! All of a sudden...*whoop*! There he was, laughing to beat the band. He got the tin alright. And me? I cut my thumb. See? See. Here."

Anna wiggled out from under the table. "Ama-ahh, let me see! I want to see too, Ama."

"Here! On the side, you see? Looks just like a little silver moon, eh? Yes — that's what I have now. That's what I'm left with now that I'm an old lady."

Anna climbed onto the old lady's lap and rested her head

against Ama's arm. She liked the warm smell of tobacco and bread and orange-scented perfume. She put her arms around Ama's neck. "Ama, tell me about the old days, okay? Please?"

Ama patted Anna's back. "Yes, yes my little one, life sure is funny, so many people died back then, in the old days. After that damned white man, he came from the outside. Me too, I lost just about everyone. It was very, very cold that one winter just after the whites came into Fort Resolution.

"We were on the river then, eh? My dad, he had built a house for us, my mama, little brother, and me. A two-story log cabin on the Little Buffalo River. We were well off. Such a big house for only four people.

"But the cold was so bad that year. Your breath would freeze in your lungs when you went outside and every time we went for water, we had to take the big axe to chop the ice. It was too hard on the river so we left.

"We had many, many relatives to stay with in the village. But when we got there...Discleneyeh. Everybody was burning up with the white man's sickness. Burning up and henhhhh...henhhhhh. No breath.

"When the snow went that spring. Heyyy. Everyone was dead. Dead I'm telling you. All the people had died through the winter. All. All. Dead.

"My mama, my papa, my sweet little brother. So many aunties and uncles and cousins. Dead."

"Ama, tell me some more, what's discleneyeh?"

"It means the devil, my girl. But you're too heavy now, get down. You want a little sip of my tea?"

Anna took her sip and slid to the floor. She leaned against the back of Ama's chair and slid her arms around Ama's big shoulders. Ama took out her hairpins. She shook out her long grey braid and rolled it back into a tight and shiny bun. She started again.

"After the whites come from the outside…"

"Where's outside? Ama. Tell me, from where they come."

"Those white people they come from all over my girl, from Edmonton, from Ottawa, from far, farrr away. Hmphhh! They're all D.P.s, those people. They don't belong here. This is *our* place, our land that they are on. We don't want their towns. Their houses and churches and their booze and their trouble.

"Oh yes. They look at us and when they want something from us, they show all their big white teeth and pretend to smile. *Lies*. Nothing but lies and back-stabbing. I know. They think because their skin is white that they are better than me but I have eyes too and my eyes they see real good. I can see that where the heart is in my body with its brown skin, there's *no* heart in those white bodies. Only greed in there. That's for sure.

"Well. I know what D.P. means, my girl. It means a displaced person. People who are where they got no business to be, I tell you. Big greedy bootlegging lying arseholes. But anyways, who will listen to an old woman like me, eh?

"Yes, those white devils came long ago and they brought their own government and their own mines and their own money and their missions. And they brought their drink. I hear booze costs the same here as it does all over the country. They make it so easy for anybody to buy it, eh? Yes, but that white grub, it costs more here, you bet! Oh, we have to fly it in they say…what do they want us to think? They want us to think the booze walks here by itself from Edmonton? Maybe it takes a dog team over the ice? They fly that in too and it's just as heavy as a box of food. They want to kill my people with that booze. They killed enough with their sickness. All my people getting sick and dying. My mama, my papa, my little brother — dead. And these days, people still dying from the drink and the arsenic in the lake from those mines and who knows what else."

Anna came around to the front of Ama's chair. She was just the right size to lay across Ama's lap with her feet still touching the floor. "But Ama. Back in the olden days…tell me more. Please."

"Yes my girl. Well, I was just a little girl like you and I was all alone in the world. The Grey Nuns, they took us into the convent. All the little girls they took. All the little orphans. Oh my God. They were mean…*strict* I tell you! Many, many tears we cried learning that French language and those prayers and that embroidery they made us do in our spare time. We had to sew all the cloths for the altar and even the robes for the priests sometimes. But those nuns, they made us work all the time, we did everything I tell you, and if it wasn't just so, just the way they wanted, we had to do it all over again. We were up at six every morning, scrubbing floors, washing dishes, helping in the kitchen, chopping kindling, washing clothes, ironing, and then on top of all that, we went to school. Oh, it was hard, hard, *hard*. But the good Lord, he pulled us through."

"And Papa, Ama, where did he come from, from the convent too?"

"Hey hey! What a notion, my girl!!! Heeheehee, from the convent! No, the boys, they had to go with the priest and the brothers.

"Yes, I remember when I met Papa, that first time. The nuns, they made all the older girls take a bath. That was something, eh? Because we had no running water and we had to carry all our water from the lake. Then we boiled all the water for washing down in the big kitchen on the old wood stoves. And then we had to carry all that hot water, pail after pail, up the stairs to the bedroom and pour it in these two big rubber army tubs. There was just one big long room, they called it a dorm, and all our beds were lined up against the walls in a row. The nuns had their own rooms on the other side of the hall. We never went in there.

"So, there was about ten of us. We were so excited, we didn't know what was going on. The only time we had a hot bath like that in the summer was for something pretty special. I was happy because my friend, that was your grandma Bertha, the nuns picked her too. So I was happy we were together. It was Saturday night, I remember. After the bath, they told us to put on our Sunday dress. We all had just three dresses, two for working, and one for Sunday. Then they made us wait in the hall upstairs. One at a time, they took us down to the parlour. They shut the door and a nun was outside, like a guard. We were a little bit scared eh? Those nuns could be so mean at times.

"When it was my turn, the nun took me in and there was Papa, all dressed up, wearing a white shirt and a tie. He was sitting straight up on the sofa. The nun made me sit beside him, and then she went to sit on a chair across from us. She just stayed like that, staring at us like a hawk and we had to sit there for half an hour. We had nothing to say to each other. We had never seen each other before in our whole lives. I was fifteen and Papa, I don't know, maybe he was nineteen or twenty. He told me he came from Hay River.

"I didn't understand. Those Grey Nuns, they kept us far away from the boys. There were some boys staying with the brothers and when they came to have the lessons at school with us, they sat on one side of the room and the girls on the other side. There was no talking back and forth. The only time we saw a man was when the priests or the brothers came to the convent. On that night, all us girls, we were up almost the whole night in our dorm, whispering among ourselves, trying to figure out what was going on. Each girl had met a different man, some old men, some young, some Indian, some white. It made no sense to us.

"Yes, those nuns! The next day, on Sunday, they gave each of us big girls a little white veil and one bobby pin. We all pinned those veils on our heads and the nuns led us into the chapel. All the men we had met the night before were waiting there. We each had to stand beside the man we met. And then the priest, he married us all at once. After, the nuns let us into the dining hall and gave us a lunch. Then we had to pack our bags and leave to follow the man they married us to. That's how I married Papa and your grandmother Bertha married old Ernest. I guess the nuns didn't know what to do with us when we were grown up. So they put out the word that if any man wanted a wife, he could come to the convent and get one. So Bertha and me and Grampa Ernest and Papa, we all came to Yellowknife together. Oh I'm telling you how I cried. Oh those tears."

Back under the table, sitting on summer. Watching the fat brown woolly legs of Mama and her friend. "My name is Black Marie, I say *Black*. You got it? My skin, look! It is black. Yup! Black Marie. I call myself that alright.

"And you and me and the Queen, our shit, it all smells the same. No matter what the colour of our skin, black, white, pink, yellow maybe. No matter how stuck up or how much money or how good you think you are, our shit all smells the same. Nobody can change that. Hmmph!"

And Black Marie would sit up real straight and stiff and put one hand on each knee and look real stubborn for a minute. Then she would grin.

Purple and bright, the navy blue skirts with woolly legs underneath. Nice socks, hot pink and day-glow lime green. Furry trim on the moccasins. Rose and wine and candy yellow flowers on Ama's toes. Patting the fur on the ankles and drifting with the fire. Listening.

WHITEHORSE, by the light of the silvery moon

Ama and Black Marie were sitting, one on each side of the oven door. The oven was open to let the heat out. Fall was coming. It was late August and in the morning all the bright outside was sparkling silver dew and the grass steaming with frost.

When you looked up, the ducks were flying across the town.

"Ehh-yah! That damned Suzanne will give me no rest till I'm dead I tell you, Marie my friend! Now she has it in her head for Anna to go up there to Whitehorse and live with her and that Tom. Yes, she thinks that she's a real big shot now, married to a white man and living in a big army house with a big fancy upstairs and hot and cold running water inside day and night. You know they even went to Niagara Falls for their honeymoon, eh? That's where all the big shots go, I hear. Who would have dreamed such a thing? The way she ran away after Louie died, leaving Anna behind. Well, she got what she was looking for alright. She found herself a brand new husband in Edmonton, now she acts all puffed up like she has the moon in her hands! A big shot. Hmph! You heard that Suzanne was in town a few months ago?"

Black Marie shook her head, frowning mightily. She liked to know everything that went on in Yellowknife. With no husband or kids of her own, she liked to keep track of all the news and it irked her to miss something as important as a visit from someone who had gone outside. The town was growing too damn big nowadays. She shifted in her chair. "Hmph!" She snorted. "Couldn't have been in town too long or I would have heard! How long was she here for, anyways?"

Anna was sitting in a patch of sunlight between the kitchen and the bedroom, playing with her doll. Her doll was all stuffed, covered with a bright pink and turquoise plaid cotton. Even the head was stuffed, to look like a pointed hood. There was a little round pompom on top of the point. The face was hard plastic with molded egg yellow wavy bangs and shiny cherry red cheeks. The eyes were painted on, two white half ovals, each with a black pie-like eye looking slyly sideways. A triangular piece of the pie-eye was painted white to show a mischievous sparkle and two tiny black tails curved at the corners for eyelashes. The red smile was like Santa Claus, droll little mouth curved up like a bow.

Mommy Suzanne had given Anna the doll when she was here. Mommy Suzanne was the nicest lady in the whole world. She was much younger than Ama, and very pretty, with rose red lipstick and black eyebrows painted on her forehead above her little brown eyes. She gave Anna so many soft warm hugs and kisses, she smiled and held Anna on her lap while she talked with Ama. When the visit was over, Anna howled at being left behind. She cried so hard that Mommy Suzanne had taken her in a taxi cab to stay over night in a tiny little room that smelled of face powder and had a suitcase full of clothes open on the chair at the foot of the bed. Mommy Suzanne put Anna in her pajamas that Ama had sent along, she brought her a piece of cake with peanut butter icing, and a glass of milk. Then she draped a fuzzy sheer pink neckerchief over the lamp and kissed Anna good night. She said she would be just outside the room having a cigarette. Anna fell asleep in a pink haze of lamp-warmed Evening in Paris perfume, and cigarette smoke. The next morning, Mommy Suzanne was in a big rush. Ama met them at the airport and Mommy Suzanne flew away in a huge noisy plane to go live with her other kids, Anna's brothers and sisters. They lived far away in the Yukon.

Ama's voice floated into Anna's patch of sunlight. "And that Tom had the kids in Whitehorse. I guess he knows lots of people there and somebody was helping him out when he went to work. How would I know anything about Suzanne's life now? She doesn't say too much to me, eh? Anyways, she was only here overnight staying at the Con Mines with those people she used to work for a long time ago. I don't know what was wrong with Anna, she was so cranky when Suzanne left that I sent her to stay with Suzanne overnight."

Black Marie stared at Anna, nodding her head. "Kids are funny, eh, Adelle? Sometimes they seem to know too much!"

"Yes, well, Suzanne, she just flew away in the airplane the next day like nobody's business and then I never heard another word from her until yesterday when I got the letter from the post office. I go maybe two, three times a week to check and see if she's sent me any word about herself, you know. She sent me pictures of all the kids and then she didn't even wait to see what I thought, didn't even ask. She just mailed me the tickets to put Anna on the airplane, and today I have to go to the priest's house to hear all about the big arrangements she's made to take my little girl from me."

Ama got up, opened the woodstove and poked at the fire to make sure it was going out and wouldn't burn the house down while she was gone.

She and Black Marie stepped over Anna to go into the bedroom. Anna watched as they got ready. Black Marie and Ama tied their kerchiefs on their heads real smooth. Ama put on her new navy blue sweater she got from the Eatons catalogue just last week. Black Marie brushed her dark purple sweater off, picking away any tiny balls of lint she thought she saw.

Ama put on her perfume that smelled like the orange icing in the biscuits from the store, she put new kleenex in her purse. Both the old ladies rubbed liberal amounts of Pond's cold cream into their hands. Black Marie was very fond of hand cream and always seemed to have a jar in her big black purse with the gold balls to clasp it shut. She let Anna snap her purse closed sometimes, it was just like an alligator's jaws. So much fun, you had to be careful not to get your fingers bitten.

Then Ama and Black Marie set off down the dirt road. They were walking to the priest's house to hear what Mommy Suzanne had to say on the telephone long distance. The priest lived just over the bridge but it was a long way for Anna to walk. Ama said she didn't want to listen to any whining today, she was just too tired and haywire.

So Anna stayed with the next door neighbours. They had a house with little bits of glass stuck in sandy green tarpaper and they had ducks, living underneath their clothes platform. All the kids were there, hanging around, looking at the ducks.

"Hey, guess what, guess what you guys! I'm going away on an airplane."

Merrill looked up from her mud pies. "Huh? Oh Yeahh you're going away, sure you're going away. Where to?"

"I'm going far away on a real big airplane to Whitehorse. That's where my real mom stays you know, her name is Mommy Suzanne. And I have two brothers, one big and one small. Yeah and two sisters too, one big and one small!"

Merrill sneered. "What's their names?"

"My big brother's name is Tommy and my big sister's name is Tina and the little sister's name is Loulou and the very smallest brother is Mickey. I'm right in the middle. That's what Ama says! And they have a real big house with a real upstairs and I bet they even have a carpet in their living room!"

Pam took her muddy fingers out of her mouth. She was Anna's best friend. "You're gonna miss school you know."

Merrill's mean little brother Chris began to dance wildly. "Hey! Anna won't have to go to school! Too bad, Anna!"

"No, I'm going to stay there forever and go to school there and everything and probably you'll never see me again, not ever, not even when I'm all grown up!"

All the kids made up their minds who was going to miss Anna when she was gone. Pam and Bobby were going to miss her. Merrill and Chris were going to be glad.

"Gee, maybe the plane will crash and then you'll be dead!"

Anna and her friends had a nice funeral and they all cried

except for Chris who laughed and threw dirt in Anna's eyes when they were pretending to bury her.

"And when I go away I'll miss everyone and write you all letters after I go to school and learn how...All except for you-know-who! So *there*!"

Mommy Suzanne sent money for Ama to buy new clothes for Anna to go on the plane in.

Anna was all dressed up in a stiff blue plaid suit, the pleated Scots skirt with shoulder straps ending in gold buttons, and a plaid hat like the old men wore, the brim sticking out in the front and a shiny gold button on the very top.

Ama braided Anna's hair tight enough to make Anna cry and then they went around to visit everyone. To show off the new clothes and tell the whole story. "Ohh yah...well, my Suzanne is doing real good now up in Whitehorse. Yes it seems she's settled down for good at last. She married a big man in the army and writes that they get along together real good. She has two more kids now. The oldest is a girl one year younger than Anna, four years old. And they have a real cute little boy too, three years old. Here, she sent this picture...see? It's in front of their place up there. Heh heh. Oh that little boy sure looks like a good one eh? Yes, she says he's a real little toughie! Likes to fight, Suzanne says! Well I guess it's the best thing for Anna to grow up there, with a father and lots of money..."

All the neighbours agreed it was for the best, but too bad for Ama. They all came to the house to drink tea and wave goodbye when Ama took Anna in a taxi-cab to the airport.

Anna flew. Over a whole world of mirror lakes and right through cold smoke in the morning clouds. She flew to Edmonton with her new colouring book and crayons and the tiny roll of fruit-flavoured lifesavers the stewardess gave her.

Some white people picked her up from the airport and took her home with them to stay overnight before she caught another plane to Whitehorse. And Anna fell sound asleep and didn't see any of Edmonton at all. She woke up only once to whooo-whoooo ooooooo and a strange room shining and the whole moon shaking. When a train went by in the big city.

And in the cold and world-without-end new morning, Anna flew again. And then there was Mommy Suzanne and a very, very big man with a moustache. He looked like a policeman. He wore scratchy, hard-looking brown pants with a big crease in them and a really starched pale green shirt with little belts on his shoulders. He never smiled at all.

Mommy Suzanne smelled really fancy. She cried and held Anna on her lap all the way home in the car. All the brothers and sisters were there too. They were very quiet.

Anna thought they must be very rich to have their own car. In Yellowknife, only the priest had a panel truck to pick up people for church. He called it Little Susie and on the way to mass every Sunday he would sing "Wake up Little Susie, wake up! The movie wasn't so hot!" Mrs. Woodburn, who was the richest woman on Latham Island where Anna and Ama lived, had a car too. It was white with big fins and red leather seats. It smelled like canned cat food and in the summer, Mrs. Woodburn would roll the top back and go really fast so the whole island behind her turned into a big cloud of choking dust.

Whitehorse was a much bigger place than Yellowknife. Most of the people were white there and they all lived in houses that looked almost exactly the same. There were red leaves and golden apple-coloured leaves like in Yellowknife, but here, rather than leaving them in glorious drifts, the people raked all their leaves into big piles and made fires out of them. There were lots more cars than in Yellowknife and there were horses too. And they even had black white people.

Mommy Suzanne laughed and said they were called Negroes. In Yellowknife, they only had one Chinese man. He worked at the Wild Cat Café.

And the house was very big. Mommy Suzanne wore fancy dresses every day, and big pink round earrings that looked like the peppermints Black Marie kept in her purse. Mommy Suzanne sang songs to Anna while she cleaned the house, "Frankie and Johnny were sweethearts. Oh the shark had pearly teeth dears and he shows them every night. Catch a falling star and put it in your pocket."

She let Anna hold the vacuum cleaner and sit on the counter to watch the electric mixer go around. The other kids got kind of mad. "How come you always let *her* do everything now huh? And we can't anymore!"

"Well, it's just because everything is new for Anna… She's not used to the way we do things up here, and we want her to feel like this is her home from now on. So be nice because she's your sister."

"We don't care, how come we have to be so nice to her! How come? She's even bigger than Mickey and Loulou and she doesn't know how to do anything we do. She's just a big spoiled baby!"

It was true. Anna cried all the time. She missed Ama. She cried when they wanted to play with her toys and wouldn't let her play with theirs. She cried when they played tag and Anna was always it. She cried when Tommy took her new doll and the arm came off. She cried when they played hide and seek and Anna was always it and couldn't find them because she got lost whenever she left the house. And when they played cowboys and Indians she was always the Indian and they would all shoot her dead. She cried when they whispered to one another and ran off, leaving her behind. And Anna always tattled and then Mommy Suzanne would pinch her lips together and look worried and sigh at Tommy who was the leader. "Just you wait until your father comes home!"

The daddy didn't seem to like Anna very much either, but then he always seemed to be mad. After he came home from work, he almost always had to scold the little boy for being mean to Anna. Everything was so strange. The daddy would get mad and shout when Anna wouldn't eat her dinner. Anna didn't like the cooking at all. It was pretty different. Mostly it seemed to be weird stuff all mixed up together in pots. Mommy Suzanne would coax…"Here, Anna, eat your nice casserole. It's sooo good…See! Mmm!…Everyone else just loves it! Even baby Mickey!"

The daddy would bug his eyes out and his mouth would go all tight. "Oh for God's sake will you quit spoiling that goddamn brat of yours!"

"Don't swear in front of the kids, and leave her alone! I keep telling you that she's not used to this food, she's been raised on bannock and fish."

And then the daddy would get really mad. *Slam*! *Slam*! "By God I have another mouth to feed and you're going on about that goddamn food you were raised on again? *Shit!*"

Mommy Suzanne had a pretty good temper. In the middle of one fight she picked up the whole platter of hot spaghetti and smiled as though she were going to serve it. Then, without warning, she fired the whole thing at the daddy's head. The fast orange noodles whizzing across the table, a rainstorm of hot salty sauce, the daddy ducking down in slow motion. The lightening crack of the oval plate against the wall, then the Chef Boyardee fingerpaint and fat long worms sliding slowly, slowly down the sun-streaked kitchen wall. All the kids said excuse me from the table please and backed out of the kitchen and ran upstairs very fast. They sat at the top of the stairs and waited. But nothing happened. The light grew deep grey and dark at the top of the stairs.

"Shh," said Tina because she was the oldest. "Shhh, don't make any noise now…"

And she mothered the other children into their pajamas and bed. "It'll be okay in the morning, you'll see, okay?" Tina hugged Anna and tucked the covers around her younger sister. Then she took Loulou into her bed.

Late that night Anna woke up. Something was wrong in the house. Loulou and Tina weren't in their bed. There was a small and scary noise. Holding her breath, Anna slid out of bed and crept out into the small hallway. All the other kids were sitting at the top of the stairs. Tina was holding Loulou very close and tight, squished up against her side. Tommy was rocking from side to side, a big-eyed Mickey on his lap.

Anna tip-toed half way down the stairs before Tina caught her pajamas and pulled her back up.

But she saw. She saw Mommy Suzanne curled up on the floor, crying and whimpering, saying, "Please, please no." And choking. The daddy was kicking Mommy Suzanne. It didn't seem very hard, but with every kick, Mommy slid a little further down the shiny, waxed, brown linoleum floor. The daddy wasn't saying anything, he just made soft little grunts when he kicked.

Thump. Uhh. The silken swish of Mommy's baby-blue nightie

sliding on the floor and his tiny grunts. Thump. Uhh.

The children made no noise at all. Tears rolled over their flushed cheeks and dripped down onto their flannel printed pajamas. Cowboys and horses for the boys, and tiny pastel pink and blue roses for the girls.

After awhile, the daddy had kicked Mommy all the way to the bedroom at the end of the hall. The door closed. Click. There were more thumping and crashing noises, but muffled and faraway behind the door.

And in the morning the very littlest brother Mickey peed on Annas face to wake her up and Tommy and Loulou and Tina were all standing by the side of the bed and giggling. Anna began to cry but Tina told her it was all Tommy's fault and hit him. Anna stopped snivelling and made up her mind to be brave. Mommy Suzanne didn't get up that morning to make breakfast. Tina helped the daddy serve cold cereal to everyone.

School started and the erasers and white glue smelled very new and nice. There was black licorice bubble gum and at recess all the boys would chase all the giggling girls. At lunch time they all went home and ate grilled cheese sandwiches and cream of celery soup. The radio played nice music, by the light…of the silvery moon. And the sun shone in the blue blue sky.

The daddy would take all the other kids roller skating and to the movies. Anna cried. "How come I can't go too?"

Mommy Suzanne crouched down and put a hand on each of Anna's shoulders. She gave her a little kiss on the forehead. "Because you're too little honey…Don't cry. Here. I'll make us some popcorn and we"ll have a nice time, just you and me, okay?"

"But Mickey and Loulou are littler than me. Mickey's only three and he gets to go."

"But Tom is Mickey and Loulou's real daddy honey. He just adopted you and Tina and Tommy. Here. I'll tell you what. We'll watch television and we'll stay up real late, okay?"

"Okay."

Anna wasn't happy at all. She cried more than ever. The daddy had to spank Anna for wetting her pants, and then Anna started wetting the bed in her sleep. She wasn't happy at all. All Anna wanted to do was go back to Ama. She didn't want to go to school or play or eat. Mommy Suzanne sent her back to Yellowknife before Christmas.

Ama was very happy.

"Here. See how skinny she is now. Feel that bony little arm! Oh the poor little thing was so homesick that she stopped eating and got sick. Well, I told Suzanne that this is where Anna belongs. I raised her from one week old. She's used to the life here with me. What do you expect anyway? Yes, she wanted to come back where she belongs. With me. No one will take her from me now."

After Christmas, Anna started grade one with all the kids she knew. They had a soft-faced teacher with a big bum covered in hairy looking skirts who was real nice and sang a song about owls that went "Tooo-whit-too-whit-too-WHOOOOOOO!"

And sandwich-spread on bannock for lunch. And the nuns teaching the ten commandments. Thou shalt not commit adultery. Thou shalt not steal. Thou shalt not covet thy neighbour's goods. Thou shalt not covet thy neighbour's wife.

"I bet covet means something dirty huh?"

And fights with Merrill to see if the kids would be her friends or Merrill's friends.

Anna was happy.

She was back home.

White Gloves and **POINTED** Shoes

After drinking tea and being stuck inside all the long and soft and muffled winter day, Ama and her friends would spread the thick grey flannel blanket on the floor, put on all their sweaters, untie their moccasins, and bring out the cards.

"Nah…here! You want some tea? Keep out of the way now eh? And be quiet for a change!"

Anna. Slow like a dinosaur. Held her mint green Fireking mug of condensed milk and tea tight with both hands. Careful, careful. A little snake without a sound and a baby egg in her mouth, she stared hard, hard at her boiling hot tea and inched her way, feet first, beneath the stove. Flat on her tummy, wiggling bit by tiny bit underneath the water boiler of the big enamelled black and shining white wood-burning stove, with its fancy iron arms curling up to hold metal shelves for steaming silver kettles and snowy warm bannock, and spruce gum bubbling thickly sticky-gold in an old tomato tin to keep away all winter sickness.

Anna wiggled slowly away from the really hot side, where thin dark sheets of caribou and moose meat with bits of lacy white fat hung drying on a straight-shaved spruce branch above the spitting, hissing, growling, orange logs.

Sipping her tea, giant woolly black and wine-coloured and navy-blue backsides hunched over before her. Mountains were sighing, settling into a tight and secret circle.

Frrp! Frrrrrp! Kings, queens, deuces, clubs, hearts, diamonds flew through fingers. There were piles of pennies by the gently steaming mugs of tea.

"Hey-heyyy Adelle, that old priest, he would be praying away tonight if he knew what was going on here, eh?"

"Ai-yeeesh what are you saying anyways? Playing for pennies is alright, eh? It's okay, not like real gambling."

"Hey-yy, my friend ... who was that one woman use to gamble all the time? You remember? Cousin to ole Chippy McDougal."

"Ohh yeahh, I know that one you're thinking of, but I think that was Florette, Maurice's wife from Pine Point, it was her that was so haywire for the cards, eh?"

"Uh-huh, uh-huh, I remember now, boy oh boy the talk was just flying around town that time, eh? Old tongues just flapping away like crazy!"

Out from under the stove, tugging at the corner of Ama's sweater. "Ama, Ama."

"What? You little nuisance."

"Ama, the story, okay? Please?"

"Ask Auntie Doris to tell the story."

"Hmmph," said Auntie Doris.

"If you ask real nice maybe." Ama lit her Players cigarette and pulled the ashtray in front of her.

Black Marie shuffled the deck, cut it, shuffled again, and dealt the cards. Anna crawled round behind the circle and tugged on the corner of Auntie Doris's sweater. The old lady shifted just a bit and a beady brown eye fixed on Anna.

"Auntie, please could you tell me the story? Please, please?"

"Hmph," said Auntie and she stared at her cards.

Anna tugged again. "Please?"

"Well, okay…for you, maybe, I guess so. A long, long time ago…"

And, like all really good storytellers, Auntie Doris stopped for a few minutes, frowning.

"Inna olden days, Auntie?"

"Nah, not that long, but a long time anyways, when you were just a little baby…"

"I'm six now."

"Eh, a big girl now eh? Okay, so maybe about five years ago then, there was this lady, see? An' she use to gamble every night."

"Like you guys?"

"No, my girl, we do it just for fun, just for pennies. But this one lady, she gamble for anything. No reason at all and she gamble away all her money, even the family allowance for her kids. She was going to have another little baby too but she gamble every night anyways. Nothing could stop that one from playing cards. She was real bad that way.

"So by'n'by she had to go to the hospital here in Yellowknife to have her little baby an ohboy! *Ohhboy!* What a time that was…nobody could look at that little baby after it was born. Not even the doctor who sees dead people every day could stay in the same room with it. So, they put it all by itself, with its mama though, eh? They put them way, way down at the end of the hall, away at the back. And they were all so scared, they sent a nurse to run for the priest.

"Quick! Quick! Come right away now they said. Yes sir, no time to lose! An you want to know something? They could hear that tiny little baby, just born, screaming and screaming when they called for the priest. It was like he knew the priest was coming, you see? So the nurses, even though they were just so scared, they went back into that room and they covered up all the windows and everything. It became blacker than night in there and they say it was freezing cold. And then the priest he came flying down the road like a big raven with his black dress all spread out behind. In his hands he was holding a crucifix from the church and a silver bottle of holy water. That water came right from the pope, I hear! Yes siree, that old priest, he wasn't fooling around, eh? An that little newborn baby, before the priest even set one foot inside the hospital door, he knew, eh. He started to scream again. Oh, it was just so awful, all the nurses covered up their ears as tight as they could.

"The whole place started to shake a little, little bit, just a little bit, and everybody, even the doctor, they went to hide around the corners when the priest walked down that long, long hall to the room. The priest, he was praying and praying, the baby was screaming and screaming, and the baby's mama was lying there ice cold with blue, blue lips. Like she was dead. Everybody was just soooo scared.

"So the priest, he stands just at the door. And he's praying away in a big loud voice, and he throws that whole bottle of holy water from Rome right on the baby. Right in the crib, I'm telling you! Yup, they say the whole place turned red lights from the baby's eyes eh? And just like throwing water on the fire, my girl, that tiny little baby, he went SSSSSS! Ssss! Sss-sss-ss!

"And right at the same time, there was *horr*-ible horr-ible screaming laughing from that little baby's mama, and they both died right in the same minute. Right then. There was such a stink. So much stink and smoke all around, that everybody ran straight out of that hospital, even the old priest. He was scared too.

"And when all the smoke went away, the little baby and his bad mama were gone. Who knows where? They couldn't find no sign of them anywhere in that whole place. Hmph. Imagine that…but that's what happens to people who gamble for money like there's no tomorrow."

Wide-eyed Anna and her tea were back beside the warm safety of Ama. "Did they go to hell, Ama?"

"Yes, my girl, the priest he told us that little baby was the devil. The devil can come anytime, you know. He could be right here in the same room with you and you wouldn't even know. But there's one sign. I'll tell you, okay? You remember this now. They say…the devil…he's always a man, eh? He can make himself so handsome. And he can talk so smooth. Oh you'll think he's just as sweet as pie. *But*. He can't change his hands or his feet, eh? So you must never just look at a man's pretty face or listen to just his words, smooth as silk. No siree. You must look hard at his feet. He has to wear big, pointed shoes to hide his hooves you see. And you must stare hard at his hands, he likes to wear white gloves to hide his big, black, hairy claws."

"Does he have a pointed tail like in the pictures, Ama?"
"Oh, I think he can hide that in his pants, my girl."
And all the ladies began to laugh so hard they choked, one by one.

ARSENIC

"Come, we're going visiting."

Ama brushed Anna's hair and braided it tight. She scrubbed Anna's hands and face with orange Lifebuoy soap until Anna's cheeks stung. Then Ama washed her own hands, and rubbed in Jergen's hand lotion. She put fresh Kleenex in her handbag, pulled on her good navy blue sweater, and tied a clean kerchief over her hair. She clicked the big padlock on the porch door shut.

"Where we going, Ama?"

"Don't be so nosy. You'll see when we get there."

They walked away from the town. The gravel road followed the shoreline of Latham Island where Ama had her house. After they passed Mrs. Woodburn's big fancy Cadillac convertible parked outside her white frame house, the road became thinner. It curved and went about a half mile up a hill through little scrubby birch and spruce trees. There were gooseberry bushes and, now and then, a raspberry bush glimmered in the piney scent. At the top of the hill, a path led off from each side of the sandy road. Anna followed her Ama on the path that led to the rocks above Great Slave Lake. The glacier-shaped rocks were smooth and round, here and there a crispy lace of grey green or pink lichens hugged a gentle curve. Moss nestled in the hollows. Here and there, blankets of tiny northern buttercups nodded sunshine-yellow heads against the luminous, grey rock.

There was a very small wooden one room house at the end of the path. One door, one window. Ama knocked and pushed the door open.

Beside the door was a playpen with a baby in it. There was a white enamel wood stove with a stack of kindling piled neatly against the wall. There were two chairs, a tiny wooden table beneath the window, a water barrel, and a bed facing the door. The room smelled of soap and smoky, tanned moose hide.

An old granny was sitting on the pink chenille bedspread, her legs tucked up underneath her. She was a very small old granny.

"Ama. Ama, why does Granny's eyes look so funny?"

"Shh! You be quiet. What a mouth! Granny is going blind, that's why. Go look at the baby now and let me talk to Granny. First, you have some manners though, go say hello."

Anna walked up to Granny and took her small soft hand. She said hello.

Granny laughed and waved her hand back and forth in front of her face. It was like the fog in the morning. Delicate brown butterfly fingers felt Anna's face, then granny patted around on the bed for her sewing basket. She took out a small tin and gave Anna a hard round white peppermint.

"Marsi cho Granny. Thanks a lot." Anna popped the candy into one chipmunk cheek and squeezed in behind Ama's chair to listen. Billy was Granny's grandson. He was grown up now. He didn't want to stay home with Granny and the baby. They tied him down. He started to drink and he swore at them when he came back from the bar. In the spring, he liked to go out on the trap line and when he came back he had money. Then he was gone.

Violette was the baby. She was almost two, and over the past few months she had learned to walk. She was fast like the dickens, and big enough to reach the hook on the door. Out the door onto the rocks where you could see the gold mines across the bay, and even over to the Indian village on the other side of the lake where they had the Ti Dances. On the high rocks with the wind and the broken bottles and the fireweeds. You could look straight down, such a long, long ways, to the lake so deep, so icy cold, so clear you could watch the seaweed waving at you.

The little path going away from the lake went straight from the door to the road where that damn white man drove so fast in his big cars.

It hurt your eyes. The sun through the window, everything was so bright. Granny liked it, she smiled and smiled. It was warm. Violette sat in the corner of her playpen sucking her arm. She only had on her undershirt and a diaper. Granny couldn't catch her anymore, she couldn't manage to dress the baby.

Ama and Granny were talking about Violette's mother and father, how they were spitting blood so bad after they came back from fishing last fall. Before Christmas they were sent outside to be fixed. No one knew when they could come back. A lot of Indians spit blood, or they had the sickness to take the breath away. Couldn't breathe, couldn't talk. Had to be taken away in the government plane to the Charles Camsell hospital in Edmonton. They talked about Ama and her old man who was crippled from spilling arsenic on his leg in the gold mine. Now he couldn't work so he fished sometimes and he was spitting blood sometimes. He kept his nets right beside the mine, where they dumped the arsenic.

Ama had kicked him out because he drank too much and made fun of the priest. Anna missed her Papa. She left her spot behind Ama's chair. She snuggled up to the playpen and patted Violette's hand through the bars. She told Violette the story Papa used to tell her after he had made her a cup of tea with lots of condensed milk in it.

"In the bush there was a bi-ig bear. Bigger than the house. A real big shot! He walked like this...*bom bom bom*! He saw some nice juicy berries. The big bear liked to eat a lot. Especially fish and berries. Yum Yum Yum. Little small rabbit was there eating all the berries."

Anna scrogled two fingers real fast together in front of her face. She hunched her shoulders way up and made rabbit teeth. Violette laughed.

"Big Bear lifted his leg wayyy up."

Anna lifted one leg to show how Papa used to lift his big leg.

"*Prrrt!!! Eeeeeeeee! Phaaa-rrrrrt!!!*

"All the little animals ran away as fast as they could. Little rabbit too. He dropped all his berries. *Thunder!!!*

Big bear laughed and laughed. He sure fooled them! He walked *bom bom bom* over to the berries. He laughed and laughed when he ate all the berries. No stink. Berries are good for you. Only big noise like thunder Phhaaaaarrt!"

Violette laughed and laughed at the noise.

Ama and Granny talked about how Granny's legs were sore because she was so old and had one foot in the grave already. She couldn't walk all the way to the store by herself with the baby. Sometimes there was no food. Granny couldn't chop wood to start the fire and heat up water to wash Violette. Granny would be okay by herself, lots of people came by everyday to help her. But the grandbaby was getting too big for Granny to take care of.

"Well, those two little angels sure look like they're getting along good, I tell you. Anna and me, we have a lot of room now with the old man gone. And we eat pretty good too. We don't live so far away, you know that. Easy for us to come back and visit anytime.

"And now Anna, she's in school all day. I could use some company. Maybe we could watch the baby until her mama comes back from outside."

Ama and Anna took Violette home with them. First thing, Ama boiled some water and gave the baby a bath in the big dish pan.

"Aii-eee, just in time. Look at the poor little thing, all lousy and scabby. Oh my lord, just look at her poor skinny little body."

Ama took her fine tooth comb and combed Violette's hair just in case. She had lots of diapers and clean clothes left from when Anna was a baby.

But the next morning, Violette was gone.

"Aaieeiiee! Find the baby Anna! Quick! Quick! No time to lose! Look by the lake! Look in the water! Anna run now! I'll go look up the road. Maybe she tried to make her way back home."

They ran looking everywhere, in the back yard, in the front yard, under the bed, behind the stove, under the warehouse, in the doghouse. Violette was nowhere.

Ama's chest was heaving. She sat down by the stove and threw her apron over her face.

"Bring me my smokes Anna, and get me the matches from the cupboard. Oh my God, my Lord, please help us."

Anna found her. Violette had stuffed herself into the very bottom shelf of the big blue food cupboard and eaten all the bannock.

"Heyy! What a big scare baby gave us, eh, Anna? Poor little thing, she must have been hungry alright to hide like that and eat nearly a whole bannock all by herself."

Anna's new sister, Violette.

Ama told the story over and over again to everyone.

CHRISTMAS Party

Instead of lunch, grades one through six at St. Patrick's Elementary school in Yellowknife, Northwest Territories, had a Christmas party. The children were lined up in the halls and herded into the auditorium where they saw the long lunch tables pushed up against the stage, covered with white paper tablecloths. Old Sister Ernestine, the convent cook, stood there holding a long fork and fishing for boiled wieners in a big steaming metal pot. She shook the water off good and hard and placed them on soft white buns next to Old Dutch potato chips on little paper plates. Sister Mary Agatha and her stinky apple breath guarded the ketchup, mustard, and relish hissing, "Just a little, just a little," as each child went by. There were real paper napkins too, bumpy white, with a faded border of green holly and three red berries in each corner.

The most exciting part came just after they began to eat. Father Fitzgerald and two of the really big boys from grade six brought in wooden cases of Coca-cola. Everyone got a whole green glassed bottle all to themselves. After eating, the children handed the empty bottles back to the nuns and filed by the big metal garbage can to get rid of the plates and napkins. They returned to the slippery grey folding chairs. At the front, Sister Mary Agatha pinned her flowing black sleeves back, cleared her throat and waved her bony little hands in the air. Altogether now, one, two, three, and all the children sang "Away in a manger, no crib for his head" and then the Huron Christmas Carol about Gitchiemanitou. Then they got to go home early.

After the hot, dizzying searches for rubber boots, crayons, mittens, homework, scarves, glue, pages to color, mukluks, ski-pants, hats, and extra socks, the nuns used their cold hard pinchy fingers to line the children up once more. The priest stood by the double front doors of the school. He handed each child a small brown paper bag of peanuts in the shell, striped fruity candy (orange, lemon, cherry, and the horrible green ones) and hard ribbon candy.

The little kids from Old Town and Latham Island had to wait for the school bus. Anna went to sit with Merrill and Christine. They were her age and lived up the street. Christine's mean little sister Kathy was there too. Anna bounced in her seat. "Hey! Guess what you guys, heyyouguys! You wanna know somethin? You wanna know somethin good?"

"Ohhh you!"

"Yeah! What do *you* want anyways? Anna banana."

"I am not."

"Y'are too...banana brain."

"Yeah. Anna's a…a *banana* face."

"I *amnot* and besides my real mom is coming to visit me tonight after school when I get home. Ama says she's just coming for tonight cause she has to go home to Whitehorse for Christmas. She was visiting in Hay River and now she's going to be here, tonight! And my big brother and sister are gonna be there too and they're real big and real strong so you guys better not call me those names no more."

"Your mom is coming? What's her name? Who's that mom you live with, anyway?"

"That's not my real mom, she just takes care of me so everybody calls her my mom. She's kind of my mom, but Mommy Suzanne is my *real* mom."

"Whaddya mean your mom, your mom, your *real* mom? Everybody else only got one mom. How come you got two?"

"Maybe cause she's Indian, that's why."

"Yeah, Anna banana gots two moms cause she's Indian. Yeah. Brown bananas. *Hey*, you get it? Brown and bananas…rahh-ten ba-naa-nas ha ha on you-ooo ha ha on Ann-aaaa."

The smell of green Palmolive soap and disinfectant. Smell of Lepages glue and chalkboard and radiators just beginning to bang on. Smell of Johnson's paste wax on the beige speckled floors and the little scratched up wooden desks. The big cold teacher with her shiny black, tied-up-tight oxfords in the big cold room.

"Now. Mother's name? Which mother? I beg your pardon. Your mother's *name* little girl. Just tell me your mother's name. Can't you understand *English*? Are you deaf or what? Are you stupid? What's wrong with these people anyway? Mon Dieu. Here, I'll start again. Now. Just tell me your mother's name."

Merrill broke into Anna's memory. "Hey, dummy Indian, wake up! How come you got two dummy mommies eh? How come your real mom doesn't want you?"

"I dunno."

"You're just too stunned eh? Hey you guys...Anna banana's so dumb, even her own dummy mommy doesn't want her!"

"Nyaa-nyaa na-na-nah. Ba-na-na-na-nah-na-na!"

"*Alright* alright already! *Enough* I said! End of the line you brats! C'mon everyone, off the bus. All of youse. *No* pushing. Don't forget your homework now hurry up by the jumpin jeeze how long ya think I'm gonna sit here with the door open? It's colder than a witches tit today! Move! Jeeze I'm gonna freeze my butt off waiting on youse." Old Carl, the bus driver, cranked the folding door open. He lit a cigarette and turned around in his seat to glare at them all.

Pushing, punching, yawning, giggling, dropping books, tripping over wet boot laces and scarves grown mysteriously long. Metal Hop-a-long Cassidy, Roy Rogers, Dale Evans lunch kits. On top of old Smoh-keyy all covered with snow I sa-aw Dale Evans without any clothes. Rainbow coloured lunchboxes silently opening in slow motion. Crumpled wax paper and bread crusts and gnawed brown apples rolling down the slushy wet aisle of the big yellow bus.

Dozy from the heat of the mile-long ride home from New Town, the children tumbled into the snow. Boys whooping and jumping at the cheek-pinching cold raced ahead. The little girls grouped together for the walk home. Snow, sparkling mauve-blue diamonds lay hushed beneath the darkening four o'clock sky.

"Boy-oh-boy, ever cold, eh?"

"Yeah an' did you hear what the bus driver said? It's a bad word, eh?"

"Tit"

"Hahaha ha ha. Tit."

"Hey, wait for Anna."

"Huh? Nahh. Let's catch up with your brothers, don't wait for her. She's too funny anyways, always makin' up stuff. Saying she has two moms."

"You don't believe her, eh? Think she's lying, eh?"

"You nuts? You wanna know a secret about her?"

"Hey you guys, wait up for me!"

"HURRYhereshecomes! Tell the secret!"

"Well, my mom an' dad won't let me go to Anna's place to play no more."

"How come?"

"You won't tell?"

"Cross my heart."

"Promise?"

"Yup."

"You better cause I'll be in trouble if my mom finds out I told."

"Oh cross my heart an' hope to die. Okay. Scout's honour. Yeah, hurryup an' tell."

"My mom won't let me go there cause they're real dirty. They don't wash or nothing."

"Everyone washes."

"No. My mom says Indians don't wash cause they don't have running water or nothing. Not even toilets inside the house. Just the night pot behind the curtain and a outhouse."

"Yeah, but they have a big water barrel in the porch and I

seen they have hot water from the stove. They have a wash stand with a basin an' towels an' everything."

"Well, my mom says they don't wash. And she knows everything. Anyways, she said Anna smells ... smells ... like the toilet!"

"You're just making that up!"

"*I am not.* My mom says those Indians stink. They're all just plain old dirty. *And* they all have lice!"

"They do? Eeeewwhhh."

"Yeah, an' you'll get lice too, if you go to Anna's house."

When the public health nurse came to school every September, all the Indian and Métis kids had to line up in the suddenly silent and shameful halls to have their heads scrubbed roughly with some lysol-smelling medicine stuff. Then they had to bend over a white cloth while one of the nuns scraped their heads with a sharp metal comb. It hurt. The white kids got to colour and play with plasticine, even the five O'Brians. Ama went to visit Winnie O'Brian all the time, bringing her Anna's and Violette's out-grown clothes and bannock and tea. She helped Winnie do the wash because poor Winnie with her good-for-nothing husband didn't even have a wringer washing machine. She only had a washboard and a square tin tub. Ama felt sorry for her.

Anna's head began to float away. To stop it, she ran past the girls as fast as she could. The boys were waiting. "Here comes Anna! Grab her!" They knocked her off the packed snow path into a snowbank.

"Hey hey you guys don't push me what are you doing*ouch*. *Don't*. Ouch. Gimme back my boot. Hey! My boots!"

"Cry baby cry-yiii."

"N-yah n-yahh yer boo-oots we got the squaw boots cry baby squaw baby ha ha on you-ooo…"

"I'm gonna tell on you guys."

The boys flew away, her brown rubber boots bouncing between them, the buckles jingling merrily. Their shouts trailed behind, down the long grey tunnel of air towards Anna. "You're not even allowed in our house, so how you gonna tell?"

"You tell an' the next time we'll pull your pants off ha ha ha!"

"An' your panties too!"

"Stupid stupid squa-aww!"

Anna floundered up through the soft, soft bed of snow, hot tears needling her eyes. The girls hustled by, giggling behind lumpy iced mittens. "Hey look, your brothers took her boots, she hasta walk home in the snow."

"Shh stop laughing it's not *nice*."

The giggles became screeches of laughter.

"Maybe her lice will get all frozen up and drop off!"

"Eeee! Hurry up! Run! Frozen lice are coming to getcha!"

Kathy walked like a big bogeyman, legs spread stiffly out and woolly claws going pounce, pounce.

"Wow, lissen to her bawling."

"Big fat baby."

"Run! Run! The lice are com-innng."

All quiet, all grey. Brittle icicle black branches snapped against the lowering evening clouds. Mountains of snow rose up to muffle the sky.

All the hushed and heavy world one pair of icy stiff socks. Waxy red and white feet. Acid blue snowflakes drifting to sleep in the cold cotton batten world.

Anna's hot pee soaking her woollen ski-pants. Tiny fairy puffs of steam, the cold heaviness during the long pin-pricking walk home. Tears formed crystal lumps on her eyelashes. Her wet chin rubbed burning raw against the frozen knitted scarf. The street lights came on as she reached the front gate. Anna began to howl.

Ama came running, wiping soapy steaming hands on her apron. Mommy Suzanne followed behind, looking very new and strange. Between big slurping hiccups, Anna sobbed out her story into Ama's neck.

"Heyy Suzanne, look what happens here in this place…those damned white brats! And their damned devil parents! They think they're so special with their big noses always stuck up in the air. Hmmph! I'm telling you it's some of their damned kids that have lice, an' it's their damn houses that smell from those chemical toilets they like so much. An' their damn yards will stink just as bad when I'm done emptying my slop in their yards all winter!"

Ama carried Anna into the house and put her on the chair by the stove. It was Ama's chair, with the shiny red plastic seat and silver legs. Ama stomped over to the corner, grabbed the slop pail and handed it to Mommy Suzanne.

"Here Suzanne, take it! Take it now I tell you! Take the slop pail right now an' go throw it over their fence. It's full enough, I think. Might as well start right away, eh? We'll see how those stuck-ups like that! An' let the sled dogs loose too, just in case they come around to say something!"

Mommy Suzanne took the pail and went outside, laughing.

Ama took off the cold wet clothes and wrapped Anna tight in a grey flannel blanket. She put a towel in the oven to heat while she rubbed Anna's feet between her hands and blew on them. Anna's feet went burning hot with a million tiny knives inside.

"Shhh, don't cry my girl, shhhh, keep your chin up now, ohh your poor little feet. At least I don't think there's no frostbite, thank the Lord." Her feet wrapped in the hot towel, Anna sat on

Ama's lap, listening to soft curses in Dogrib. Curses against the damn D.P. white man.

She stared at the room full to bursting with brand new bright blue shiny metal suitcases and stiff green canvas sacks. Mommy Suzanne blew back in the room bringing cold air that smelled of Evening in Paris perfume. She looked pretty white. And pretty rich too. She was wearing nylons with the black line up the back and sparkly golden rubber high heeled boots, buckled tight with shiny white nylon fur all around the ankles. Her turquoise wool suit looked just like the one Mrs. Green the welfare worker wore. Her bangs were curled like a fat black sausage and the bottom of her hair was rolled up tight around her neck. She had red, red lipstick and big long yellow teeth when she smiled at Anna. Her eyes were nice. They looked like little boiled raisins.

Violette crept out of the bedroom where she had been hiding. She was very shy. She came and stood behind Ama's chair. Both she and Anna stared at the older brother and sister. Tommy and Tina stared back, sitting across the room on the edge of the cot underneath the little shelf with the statue of the Blessed Virgin Mary, their feet dangling. No one smiled.

Anna thought they looked very nice even though she couldn't remember them very well. Two years ago, when Anna was starting grade one, and Tina and Tommy had been in grades two and three, Ama had sent Anna up to the Yukon to live with them. All she remembered was the baby brother Mickey peeing on her head to wake her the morning after really a lot of screaming and thumping from downstairs where Mommy Suzanne and the scary daddy slept at night. Mommy Suzanne had sent her back to Ama before the snow fell. Anna looked back at Mommy Suzanne, then she whispered to Ama.

"Where's Loulou and Mickey?"

Ama looked at Mommy Suzanne. "Who's been taking care of your babies while you were visiting your friends in Hay River all week, Suzanne?"

"Oh Ama, they've been alright. They're in Whitehorse with Tom, too young to travel yet, you know. The neighbour has three kids of her own and she's been watching them while Tom was at work. Besides, we'll be home tomorrow night, in time for Christmas. It's still three days away. You should see the cute little doll I picked up for Loulou in Edmonton, Ama! Susie-so-soft it's called! I'll show you later, okay?"

Then Mommy Suzanne bent over the stove and made big sniffing noises. "Boy-oh-boy that smells so-oo good, Ama! What's in the oven? Hey-heyy good-lookin, whaa-cha got cookin?"

"Ai-yeesh! What silliness! But I had such good luck a few days ago, I'm telling you Suzanne. Just when I finished sewing all those mukluks for the Indian Agent I heard the news. The same day! That Indian Agent, he gave me twenty bucks a pair for those mukluks. So there I was walking home with my purse just full of stumpa and I ran into Mrs. Devereaux. Her Jimmy had just come from hunting the night before. He killed two big moose. So I rushed right over to the Peace River Flats an' I bought some. That's the head cooking now!"

"Ooh la-la!" crooned Mommy Suzanne. "C'mere kids! Take a look at this. Sure smells good, eh? We never have anything this good to eat in Whitehorse. I tell you, Ama, I live just like a white woman. There's this one woman last summer. Sure was a mean old bitch, pardon my French, eh? She comes over to me on her big high heel shoes one day, tap tap. Her nose is way up high in the air, but she's pretending to be so friendly and nice. Just nosy though, I could tell. "My!" She says to me "My goodness, Mrs. Morris, your children have such *lovely* tans this year, and they tan so fast, too!"

"They all think I'm white up there in Whitehorse you know. They must be half-blind. Little Loulou with her curly hair, she looks like a beach ball from the top. And her skin turns just black in the summer! I'm telling you, she looks like a little blond Negro! She sure is pretty, you've never seen anything so cute in all your life.

"Well, anyway, this woman I was telling you about, she knew something was up, eh? She was trying to figure out if I was Indian. I laughed so hard when she asked me about those tans I almost peed in my fancy dress. A nice tan! Yes, my kids do have lovely tans I'd say to her and I'd look real innocent. I guess we're just lucky! Tom doesn't seem to want anyone to know me and the kids are half-breed, eh? Who knows? Maybe it would look bad because he's in the army.

"I put up with it Ama, I play along. I think it's no one's business but my own, and I don't like nosy people. Besides, Tom is okay. He's a good provider for the kids, and they need a dad, eh? He's just crazy about me he says. It gives me a kick anyway. I can act just like those white women, you know, when I want to. Those white people, they don't like anyone to get too close to them, they like to keep to themselves. They have so many rules for everything, Ama! You can't just go drop in on your neighbour up there. Oh no. You have to telephone first and ask what's a good time to visit? Two o'clock you say? Perfect! See you later, alligator! So every day I put on a dress, some high heels and big fancy earrings. I put on pancake make-up and perfume. Pretty please this and how-do-you-do that! If only they knew, eh, Ama?"

Ama said nothing, she just looked at Mommy Suzanne. She was frowning, just a little bit. Violette and Anna stared with all their might.

All the time she was talking, Mommy Suzanne was taking dishes out of the wooden turquoise cupboard and setting the table. With the roasted moose head they had boiled potatoes saved from Ama's summer garden in the back yard. Ama had made a bannock, nice and crispy on the outside with butter melting into the soft and floury middle. For a special treat for the kids, Ama heated up an expensive can of the little cubed carrots and peas. The women divided the tender sweet moose cheeks between the children. They all shared the tongue next. Tina and Tommy weren't used to moose head and they didn't want to eat the chewy meat from the eyes. Mommy Suzanne laughed at them and said it was about time she brought her kids back to the bush.

Mommy Suzanne and Ama kept telling stories and the children just looked at one another. Tina and Tommy wriggled their chairs close to each other. Anna and Violette were glued to Ama's skirt.

After supper, Ama plugged in the lights of the Christmas tree by the door. She had put the kettle on to boil while she and Mommy Suzanne washed and dried the dishes. They pushed all the suitcases and duffel bags into the bedroom.

The children were still shy, looking at each other, then at the tree, and then at each other again. Anna brought out her bag of Christmas candy and peanuts from school and finally just when they all began to have fun looking at the ornaments and playing with the little plastic manger under the tree, it was time for bed.

Mommy Suzanne watched Tina and Tommy wash their pale,

pale faces and brush their tiny white teeth. She took clean, cold pajamas out of the shiny blue suitcase. Ama unrolled the sleeping bags from under the table and shook them outside in the fresh cold air. Then she hung them over the pole by the stove to warm. She dragged the extra mattress from under her bed and put it in front of the little round wood stove in the bedroom. The sleeping bags were put down, a clean striped flannel sheet and pillow tucked into each one. Tina and Tommy went to bed.

Violette was washed, put into her nightie and tucked into the big brown crib at the foot of Ama's bed. Anna was put to bed too, instead of sitting under the table in her usual spot until she fell asleep. A heavy wool blanket was folded in half and strung up between the two rooms.

Anna looked over the edge of Ama's big iron bed at Tina and Tommy. They didn't move. She looked over at Violette. Violette was snoring softly, her fat cheeks flushed with the heat from the stove.

Anna held her breath and wiggled slowly off the bed. She took her bag of candy and crept behind the blanket to watch. It was very exciting. More and more people kept crowding into the front room, stamping the snow from their mukluks, and snapping their mittens against the door frame.

Mr. and Mrs. Blanchette came, with their daughter Rosie who was like a movie star in a fancy mink fur coat. Old Karl was there with his big cane, and Black Marie and T'Atiste from next door sat in the corner, watching. Everything was bright and hot and smoky and loud. People laughing, sweating, their shining faces, sitting on each others laps and on the floor and on the table. Everything smelling strong of home brew and cigarettes and hair dressing. Ama plugged in the record player, and after it had warmed up, she played her record over and over again, with the dial turned up high as it could go.

Poor little raw-ah-bin
walkin, walkin, walkin, to New Or-leens
and
Laven-derrs bloooo, dilydilly, laven-derrs bloo,
Poor little raw-ah-bin, walkin, walkin,

Whoever heard of a robin walking? And to New Orleens...must be outside, New Orleens.

Anna's head slowly heavy, sliding down the door frame she was propped up against, her candy coming unstuck from fuzzy fingers.

New Orleens, was it as far as Edmonton? Who broke the robin's wings? Maybe that's how his heart got broken, too...Must have been a pretty strong woman for sure, to throw a rock hard and fast enough to break a robin's wings *and* his heart at the same time. Mean too. She must have had a twenty-two. That was really the only way to get that robin. Must have been white too. No Indian woman would shoot a robin. They were too small for eating, everyone knew that.

And what was lavender, purple stuff...belonged to kings and queens. Only English people in books said dilly dilly.

"God DAMN you fucking cocksucker! You cocksucking white asshole! COCKsuck-ERRR! BASTARD!"

Anna jerk heartTHUMP! Eyes popped wide open. Her throat closed up tight. Record player k-k-k-hrrrrsh kac kac kac kac. She peered from behind the blanket. Everything and everyone was moving too fast. In the blur, robin shattered into shiny licorice black shards. Everyone was noisy. Mommy Suzanne was swearing. She ripped the tree from its lard pail holder. The warm Christmas smell of pine filled the house.

The door was banged open and a strange man ran out of the house without his coat. Waving the little tree, Mommy Suzanne followed. She was pretty fast with her high heels in the snow. Ama burst out the door next, pulling her sweater on. All the people crowded around the door to watch.

Anna ran to the bedroom window to watch her Ama chasing her Mommy Suzanne chasing a man down the road.

The tree twinkled through the blue indigo night. A million snowdrifted diamonds sparkled under the street lamp. A trout tail of nursery rhyme lights swam behind the Christmas tree. Humpty Dumpty and Little Boy Blue. Curses and magic ornaments flying. Bright flashing reindeer and fuzzy-haired angels, Santa Claus and the Christ child glued to his manger crushed into starlight, shattered against the sugarplum snow.

There was drunken laughter and cheering from the doorway.

"Haw haw haw haw! That'll teach that white guy to come around like he own's the place! That'll teach him to keep his big dirty mouth shut!"

Anna's heart blew up in her chest. She looked at Tina and Tommy, their eyes scrunched tight shut, so frozen quiet she knew they were awake. She flew across the room and back into bed, pulling the quilts up way over her head. The pounding of her heart drummed her softly to sleep.

T'ATISTE

There were three big rocks just outside the front door. They were close to each other, in a semi-circle. It was a nice sunny day, and right after breakfast Ama, Anna, and Violette had painted all the rocks blue, the same colour as the Virgin Mary. Later on, Mrs. Dryfat was passing by and she stopped to admire them. Ama made a little fire just in front of the rocks and boiled some water. Now they were sitting on a blanket next to the rocks, drinking tea, and talking about T'Atiste. Violette and Anna were taking turns on the swing nearby.

Next to Black Marie, T'Atiste was Ama's other good friend. She lived right next door with her husband Joe. They had a grown daughter named Rose, but she and her husband were never around. In the winter they were out on the trap line, spring and fall they went hunting, and in the summer, they were fishing. Rose and her husband had five children. They had all been taken away and put into the residential school in Fort Smith. The parents got their kids back in the summer and sometimes they all came to stay with T'Atiste. T'Atiste was very proud of her daughter and grandchildren. T'Atiste and Joe also had a grown son. His name was Ronald but everybody called him Ronnie, and he stayed with them all the time.

Ama was talking. "A real good for nothing, that one...Hmph! With his hair all greased up like that he sure thinks he's something. Sometimes I see him walking down the road with his nose in the air like a big shot. And I'm telling you, I have to step out the door and take a real good look to make sure that's his head on top of his body there and not the frying pan floating along the road. So black and greasy!"

Mrs. Dryfat laughed and laughed. "Oh Adelle! So sarcastic! He he heee, you're right for sure though, hmph. He's no good! And such a good mother, too! You know, I hear that Ronnie he goes drinking for days and days, and then he just comes home when he hears that his poor old mum, she has a bit of money. Then he beats her up and takes it away."

Anna and Violette watched Mrs. Dryfat spit her chewing tobacco into the spittoon by the fire. She had a good aim and was really fast.

Ama fixed the two little girls with her serious look. "You kids stay away from him, you hear? He's a ba-aad one. They say one time he was down by the water on the dock. It was a nice day just like this one, only later on, in the evening. The sun was just going down, it was in the spring, I think eh?" Ama looked at Mrs. Dryfat for confirmation.

Mrs Dryfat pursed her lips and nodded in agreement. "Spring."

Ama went on. "So anyways, he's down there by the lake, pretending to be such an innocent, and you know what he's doing? Calling. Calling for the devil to come to him so he can sell his soul and have money to go to the Ol' Stope and drink some more. So he can get stumpah to go and gamble some more. And the devil came for sure that time. Nobody could see him except for Ronnie of course, but they knew he was there all the same. That no good Ronnie was standing at the edge of the dock, waving his hands and talking out loud to Satan. They were making a deal you see, Ronnie would win all he wanted to at cards, but the minute he died, the devil would reach out with his big long scaly fingers and grab Ronnie's soul like that!" Ama clapped her hands together sharply to show how fast the devil would take Ronnie's soul.

"Yes, yes," Mrs. Dryfat nodded. "The devil, he came for sure. He knows that damn Ronnie alright. Oh, I would be so scared to die if I was that Ronnie. Just imagine you would be laying there on your death bed when you're old. And who would be the one sitting there with all his big stink choking your last breath? Sitting in the chair right beside your head? A big hairy devil, that's who! Satan himself will come up from the fires of hell. He'll be laughing away at poor Ronnie. Time to keep your end of the bargain now he'll say. Time to keep your word! Your Ama's right. You kids stay away from him. Who knows what somebody like Ronnie will do to a kid? Errrr, what a snake he is. Poor T'Atiste! The white man's drink has sent another one to the devil." And Ama and Mrs. Dryfat looked solemnly at each other while they both made the sign of the cross over their chests.

"Poor T'Atiste, what a good-hearted woman to put up with a grown son like that, but she'll never say even one bad word about him, eh? Just keeps working away and helping her old man and her daughter, taking care of all those grandkids. And the way she keeps that house clean. I'm telling you, she doesn't even need a table, those floors are clean enough to eat right off them."

"Hmph! That's true," said Ama. "But I think she should go to the church once in a while though, to pray for that Ronnie!" Ama thought everyone would be better off if they went to church three times on Sunday and said the rosary every night. Mrs. Dryfat was very polite. She just smiled at Ama.

"Hey Adelle, you smell something? I think it's coming from T'Atiste's place."

Ama and Mrs. Dryfat stood up and walked over to the red picket fence. They stood there like two book-ends with their braided heads turned and tilted in exactly the same way. They peered down the little hill to T'Atiste's house. Anna and Violette climbed the steps to the clothes platform so they could see better. There seemed to be a wisp of smoke curling over the roof from T'Atiste's backyard. Something smelled really good.

Mrs. Dryfat leaned as far as she could over the fence and breathed in deep. "Smells like she's smoking some fish, eh? I bet she's making a bannock to go with it. What do you think, my friend?"

Ama watched the wood smoke float up to meet a fat little puffy cloud. "I think I'd sure like a nice piece of fresh fish smoked a little bit and grilled over the fire! Oh boy! Maybe T'Atiste wouldn't mind some visitors today!"

Ama and Mrs. Dryfat hustled back to the blanket. Ama was in such a rush she didn't even fold the blanket, she just snatched up her smokes and put them in her apron pocket. "You kids stay home now. Anna, you keep a good eye on your sister. Don't let Violette go on the road. What do you say if someone comes to the door while I'm gone?"

"Ama le tea attunh, and then we point the way down the hill to T'Atiste's place."

"That's right. Now you be good while I'm gone and no fighting, you hear me? And don't follow me like always. Just like little puppy dogs sometimes!" And Ama sped out the gate to spend another afternoon in the house next door that smelled like sunlight bar soap and sweet grass baskets.

After awhile, Anna and Violette followed her as they always did, creeping through the bushes by the fence in case Ronnie and the devil were lurking near by. Just waiting to pounce. Ama and Mrs. Dryfat and T'Atiste were sitting in the teepee that was put up every summer to smoke fish.

Fat fish split into butterflies, with the flesh cut across into soft golden ribbons, were hanging from slim poles stretched above the small fire in the centre of the teepee. Fresh and springy pine branches were spread around for the floor.

The women were sitting on grey wool blankets placed on the branches. A sequinned rainbow of tiny colours glittered in front of them. They were helping T'Atiste sort out translucent pink and yellow needles into squat glass jars.

Ama saw them first.

"Hey you kids, come in here and take a look at this. This is something you won't see every day. Just take a real good look at this."

The little girls went into the beautiful tent. Went into the head-spinning scent of fresh pine and sun bleached canvas and smoked white fish. Wood smoke glowing cerulean blue against the golden walls and the little blue and orange flames shimmering against the velvet brown earth in the middle.

"Hol-eee! Look Violette! What are they, Ama?"

"Porcupine quills. Sure not too many people left who can do a good job making them like this anymore. Look at all the colours, just look. And look what else T'Atiste got too!" T'Atiste proudly held up a fat round glass jar that shone like every jewel ever told about in any fairy tale. She laughed shyly and gave Violette the jar to look at closely.

"Fish," she said.

"Fish?" The girls looked at Ama. "Fish?"

"Yes, dyed porcupine quills and dyed fish scales for embroidery on moccasins. In the olden days before everybody started to use those beads from the store, this is what we used for embroidery. Take a real good look, eh? Who knows when you will see something like this again!"

T'Atiste carefully wrapped up the jar of dyed fish scales in a bit of deep purple silk and put them away in her big black felt sewing bag with pinked edges. With orange, peach and candy-pink flowers and spearmint coloured leaves sewn all over in silk thread. She gave Violette and Anna one porcupine quill each and the girls pretended they were porcupines. They made such a headache for the women by jabbing each other and screaming, that they were very quickly pushed out of the tent.

They sat forlornly on the rock in front of T'Atiste's doorstep, the one Ama had persuaded T'Atiste to paint turquoise and gold. Ama had wanted to see how those rocks would look before she painted her own.

Violette snuffled at the scolding they had received and Anna counted the number of pointed wooden paddles leaning against the wall of the house. Each paddle had an inside-out muskrat skin stretched tightly over it to dry in the afternoon sun.

After a bit, T'Atiste, who had the softest heart of the three women, came out of the tent. She gave Anna and Violette some hot bannock and smoked fish on little white and blue enamelled plates. She gave them each a big tin mug with tea and condensed milk in it.

Let's **PRETEND**

The white kids wouldn't play with Anna because she was a half-breed and she lived in the poor part of Yellowknife. With her grandmother. Well. Where were the parents, then?

The Indian kids were shy. Anna looked too white.

The other Métis children thought she was crazy from living with an old witch who prayed all the time. Whenever she wasn't drinking.

Anna lived in dreams, she lived in books, she lived in the roots of the birch tree in the front yard and drank tea from hollowed out rosebud cups. She smoked a fireweed stem pipe.

Close your eyes now.

The cool wormy earth cut through by birch leaves true and green and sharp. Crispy sheets of lacy pink, grey green, gold and orange lichens like small shawls hugging the rocks. The smell of

Precambrian loam, fat brown and green moss cushions nuzzling into the sharp pastel hollows of rock.

Anna crushed tiny leaves to her nose. Put them in her mouth and chewed. She was walking down the dirt road with baby nubs from spring trees lacing over her head. Like a grotto, thought Anna.

She was a Greek saint.

She was blessed.

She lived in Wales and could dance like a loon. Sing like a chickadee.

Anna lived far away down south in the United States in a plantation house with great white pillars and sugar growing right by the front walk.

She was in Ireland and following a leprechaun-ridden rainbow. She was going to visit the new kid that had moved to the old town.

The new kid was in grade five too.

Everyone teased her. Because she was a bohunk. What's that? A kid with a face golden as a saint in the bible, who talked funny but nice, wore green buckled shoes and thick hand knit brown stockings. The kid had a funny name, and an even funnier mother who talked in a really different way.

But oh.

Could the funny mother ever cook. When Anna walked in the door, the whole little house was lit up like Christmas with the hot smell of jam in butter-melted pastry.

"Hey Alexandra, is your mom in the kitchen? Let's go see her and tell her I'm here okay?"

Holding onto each other, the two little girls peered around the corner of the door frame at Mrs. Lowinski.

"Oh, Ahna, you came to play? Come in, come in, and don't be shy. Here. Have a piece of this."

"What's it called? Ever goo-ood."

"Zomezink from za old country…linzertorte. Say it Ahnah…lin-zer-torte. Zat's right. Keyy-rect. You got it."

Linzertorte.

And after the linzertorte and after cutting out all the paper doll clothes and all the tiny high heels that always bent. After the finger numbing tiaras were done and fitted on the funny faced paper doll with the yellow helmet hair, long noodly legs and icing-pink underwear.

Anna and Alexandra played with the little brother's plastic soldiers. It's a war, it's a war. And they threw all the tiny red and yellow and blue cowboys forever stuck with horses between their legs. Threw the generals, Indian braves, tanks and cannons around the room in a thunderstorm, with wild howlings coming from little brother.

Then Mrs. Lowinski came in. She looked. Left. Came back with a green felt hat on her head and a large paper bag in her hands.

"Come now. Time for zome fresh air, I zink."

They all climbed up high the rocks behind the house. Climbing to the hawks and ravens, to the water tower at the very top where they could see the lake below with the big boats tied at the wharf.

"Whuffff…I am too old I zink. Hoooooo! Too old and too much good cooking. But. Vot za hell. Tch."

Mrs. Lowinski sat down on a big rock to catch her breath. They all looked past the boats to the little island.

Anna pointed. "Look! I can see the Llewellan's house! Can you see?"

The Llewellans lived in a white-painted wood house on the small round island. They rowed across to the wharf when they needed to buy stuff from the Weaver and Devore store.

Ama sometimes got hold of a canoe from somewhere and she and Anna and Violette would paddle over for a visit. The house was nice. It had a real bear skin on the wall over a stone fireplace and the couch had a wool blanket knitted out of brightly coloured little squares all sewn together.

Anna and Violette thought the house smelled like sick mans guts, but Ama scolded them when she caught them pinching their noses. "Dice-lean-yehh!!! Can't take you little devils anywhere eh? What a shame you are! It's only the chemical toilet you smell. White people have those. Don't like to go outside in the wintertime. Too soft! You should know that by now! Be polite. Stop it now before she sees you, ssssss."

Mrs. Llewellan was really old. Her face was all wrinkled up and her hands shook most of the time. Just a little bit, though. She baked a cake with bright green lime-flavoured icing. It was pretty good and the garden had cheese whiz coloured day lilies and little scarlet flowers shaped like frilly trumpets. Anna and Violette bit the bottoms off and sucked out the sugar juice.

Ama always got something from Mrs. Llewellan's garden. Some baby carrots or new potatoes or a bunch of purple pansies. To stick in the vase that was attached to the back of the holy Virgin Mary and sat high on a special shelf at home. The Virgin Mary looked like a baby blue hunchback. When Anna grew up, she would be a doctor and fix that back.

"Hey Alexandra, you wanna know something funny?"

"What's that?"

"When we was over visiting the Llewellan's place last time,

Mr. Llewellan was taking a real, real long time in the toilet, eh? Violette almost wet her pants waiting…you shoulda seen her wiggling around. Holee crow! Anyways we went and asked Mrs. Llewellan how come Mr. Llewellan took so long and you wanna know what she said?"

"What?"

"She sa-id. That Mr. Llewellan is real old, even older than her, eh? An he's got a dis-eease an he's real sick…" Anna paused for effect. "So when he goes…you know…number two? All his guts fall out his bum an' he has to take a real long time to poke them all back inside really careful. He even has a special stick he keeps right by the toilet to poke his guts back inside with!"

"Cheeeeee…mein gott mein gott in heaven. Vat are you saying, child? You stop zat gossip right now this minute if you want zomezink to eat. Go gadder me zome sticks for za fire. Mein gott." Alexandra's mother stood up from her rock. She took some fat sausages out of her shopping bag.

The children scattered, whooping and jumping over the rocks. Gathering twigs.

While the sausages were roasting, Alexandra told her mother about Anna. How Anna said she could pump so hard on the swings at school that she went right around the bars. Three times. And she flew off the swing and landed on her brother. Crunch. And broke both his arms. And how Anna lived in the biggest house on Latham Island. With a tower and coloured glass windows like you saw in church. Anna had her own room as big as the classroom at school, with a double bed and a big quilt soft as feathers with pink flowers and violets on it. There was even a window seat with a fat purple bunny rabbit on it. The rabbit had a wide shiny yellow ribbon tied in a big bow around his neck.

And whiskers too. Alexandra's mother laughed so hard, she started to fall off her rock.

"Ohhhhh stop! pleeeease! Oh. Vat a liddle liar your new friend is, Allessandra! Vat a liar! Vat a head she has. She zinks too much. She sees too many pitcher books I zink. Oh! Ha ha ha haaa! A half-breed kid vat zinks she is liffing in a big vite house. Wiz pillars! Oh ha haaaaa ha ha ha ha."

Tears in her eyes, Anna glared and scuffled her feet.

"If you were my kid, I vould giff your mouse a real good vash wiz Lifebuoy soap!"

Anna turned red. She lived in books, in dreams, in tangled tales. She remembered the mornings at school. The radiators hissing. The big important teachers.

"Anna. Get up here and tell the rest of the class what you have for current events."

Scuffling to the front of the classroom. Stomach in her mukluks. Heart going bumba-bumba. "Well. On the radio when I was eating my porridge..."

"Ann-nnna. We're not interested in your breakfast are we class?"

Thunder. No Miss Whitely. Titter. Chairs scrape. Head blowing up.

"I heard about how the Russians are going to bomb the DEW line but first they want to kill us but first they wanted to find out where we were so they went to Edmonton to get a monkey it's too cold in Russia, just like here anyway. They ran out of monkeys at the zoo but that was okay cause in Edmonton they have guys with big moustaches standing round on all the corners and their monkeys play the organ and..."

"Whoaaa! You heard this on the radio, did you, little miss?"

"Yeah honest! And then the Russians were tryin' to..."

"Anna. We all listened to the radio this morning too. And did any one hear this news?"

Thunder. No Miss Whitely.

"For punishment Anna, you can stand in the corner. Again."

"I can't honest. Ama took me to the doctor yesterday and he said I have polio. And my back really hurts. I think I have a fever too."

Shocked looks.

"Now class, let's all tell Anna how we have things wrong with *us*!"

Ha ha I have a headache heee hee a toothache. I have...aha ha ha. My foots frozen off. Look. Me! No. Me! Earaches. Ha ha ha. I have a toe ache. Haw haw haw.

The class had a lot of fun. Anna stood in the corner until recess.

Mommy SUZANNE

Anna was kneeling on the turquoise painted chair by the front window. She was scraping frost pictures on the glass and sucking the ice shavings from underneath her fingernails. Black Marie's gypsy flowered kerchief hustled above the snowdrift in front of the red picket fence out front. A big white bundle floated in front of the kerchief. Bang, bang on the porch door.

"Ama-aa! Black Marie's banging on the door! She has a big parcel in her hands!"

"Tsk! What a nuisance, this hook!" Clunk! Clunk! Pieces of chopped firewood stored in the porch falling on Ama's moccasined toes. "Disclenyeh!" Ama's soapy hot hands steaming and slipping, fumbling to open the two doors in the porch. Two doors to lock against bogeymen and the cold and drunks and nosy white folks. "Oh what luck to see you today Marie! Come in, come in, my friend. Nah! Here! By the stove where it's nice and hot. I'll put some more wood in for you to warm up fast. Sit down while I finish this washing, it won't take me long."

Blowing and puffing and snapping her rubbers. Unwinding the braided mitten strings and the bright woolen tassels and shawls and scarves and sweaters blowing about in an icy cold breeze of snow and the scent of Pond's wild rose hand cream.

"Whoof! What a job, Adelle! I brought you some dry meat here, my friend! And I have lots of big news today for sure . . ." Black Marie stopped short, squinted her shiny black eyes at Anna. "How come you're home? No school? You sick? Disclenyeh! You stay far over there if you're sick! Me, I'm too old for that!"

Anna had the whooping cough. She liked it. It was nice staying home from school all wrapped up in hot towels and wearing flannel pajamas all day. Reading books. Nancy Drew and Trixie Beldon and Wuthering Heights. Listening to the radio. Love and good wishes between all the people in the north. From Jim in Coppermine to his sweetie you-know-who down south in Hay River. I got a feeling called the blooooooh-ooohs. Oh lard, I think I'm gonna dieeee. Scary CBC plays about crazy farmers in Saskatoon who hugged people to death and then were murdered with a pitchfork. Followed by "Gather Round" and "Country and Western Roundup". It wasn't God who made honk-eee tonk aaa-angels. And now we have George Szell and the Cleveland orchestra with Dvorak. Four Slavonic Dances. And here is "A Child's Christmas in Wales" by Dylan Thomas. And now for an oldie but goodie folks, that old smoothie himself, Perry Como. Catch a falling star and put it in your pocket, never let it fade away.

Ama grumbled over the wringer washer to Black Marie. "This

one is always the one to get sick. Every night now she sits up in the bed like a jackrabbit. Anytime! Three o'clock in the morning I tell you and whuff all over the sheets. Just before you knocked on the door, I was in luck. I see her start whoop, whoop and I grabbed her skinny little legs and held her upside down over the slop pail. Yes sir, with her head right inside. She's so big now, it was hard, but I managed. Whew. Just in time too! I'm washing, washing, every day now."

Ama pointed with her chin to the corner. The new baby was asleep in his swing. The swing was made out of a soft blanket folded over on itself between two ropes. It hung over the folding cot that Ama kept for sick people who had no place to stay while they were waiting for a plane to take them outside to the hospital in Edmonton. Sometimes, the same people came back after the hospital and waited for another plane to take them back to where they lived. There were a lot of babies that came and went.

"This baby, I think I'm going to keep him. Now he's back from hospital, and his parents are out in the Barren lands. No one can find them. He sure is good-natured, laughs all the time. Anna and Violette like him too. Name's Harry."

Black Marie started to unwrap her parcel. She sorted out the dry meat into two piles on the table. "Hey Adelle. Another kid? He likes to eat? Looks too young for dry meat though."

"I'll pound it nice and fine for him, make little meatballs with fat and then roll them in sugar. He has lots of teeth now and tries to bite everything. Anyways, we got room now for another kid. Violette is going to school, and I need some company in the day. You'll see! It'll work out good."

"Hmph. Well, he's sure big enough!" Black Marie poked the

swing and set it rocking gently, then she sat down on the edge of the folding cot and leaned forward in a big excitement. She smacked her two hands down onto her fat knees.

Anna stopped scraping the window. She knew how Black Marie sat when she had big news.

"Guess what, Adelle! Suzanne, she's back in town again and she's sober! Honest to God. Cold sober all the time now! She's looking for a place to stay. Tom, he gave up on her. I hear he took his kids back to Ontario. Tina and Tommy, they're in the hostel in Fort Smith. The welfare took them away for good now, I hear. I guess that sobered Suzanne up for a little while. Heyy Adelle, she was a good woman when she wasn't drinking, you know that, Maybe you need some help with the new baby boy?"

"Hmph!" Ama slapped the wet clothes into the basket to hang out on the line.

Black Marie wouldn't give up. "Adelle, what can you do? You have to take her in, you know that! She's like your own blood."

"Hmph. You say she's sober now eh? No drinking?"

Black Marie pinched up her face and squinted her shiny slit eyes at Ama, "You think I'm lying to you? My old friend?"

Ama shot a lightening sharp glance at Anna. She put down the wet sheets and went over to the window. She grabbed Anna's shoulder and pushed her to the bedroom. "You go in the other room now. Time for a sleep."

Ama shoved Anna into the bedroom and watched her climb under the quilt. She took the poker and stirred up the fire in the bedroom stove that was made from an old oil drum. As soon as Ama's back was turned, Anna was sliding out of bed to crouch by the door frame and listen.

Ama went on. "Well, that Suzanne, I heard she's had a lot of trouble, eh? The first husband shot so long ago, and now Tom leaves her because of that devil bottle. Now a brand new heartache. What happen with that fire in Fort Smith, anyways? I heard they passed out and the oil stove blew up while they were sleeping. Is that true? Did anyone get hurt? Did you hear any news about that mess?"

Ama counted on Black Marie. She always knew everything that went on. Everywhere.

Black Marie shook her head from side to side. "Aiii-eeee, it's *bad*! Bad, Adelle! He's gone. He died in the fire. Suzanne, she got along with that man real good. Nobody ever seen her so happy for a long time. She stopped drinking so much, and took care of the kids. It's been awhile since Tom left now eh, and she was on her own for too long. Stop being so hard-hearted, my old friend. You shouldn't be so hard on Suzanne all the time. She loves her kids, you know that. She just can't help herself with that drink anymore. It makes her so haywire now."

"Eh, Marie! What are you saying? If that man was so good and she loved him so much, they should have been married in the church, not living like dogs. Aii! What am I saying anyways? I must be losing my mind my own self to say such a blasphemy! That old Pope only lets you get married one time in that Roman Catholic church. And now, she's on her third man. Shacked up right in front of the kids, too. No shame. Is that true?"

"Hmph! Don't believe everything you hear, my friend. You know damn good there's people in this town look for the worst in everything! Me, I never heard nothing bad about Suzanne, honest to God."

Black Marie and Ama started whispering and hissing like a couple of fat brown snakes. Anna glared at them from behind the curtain that hung in the doorway. She couldn't hear a thing.

It seemed like a real long time passed before Ama moved away from Marie. She started to make tea.

"And you say Suzanne is sober? After that? Disclenyeh."

Black Marie sucked her teeth. "Tss! Well, she hit the bottle pretty hard for awhile. Sure she did. But I tell you, she's okay now. I saw her in the Hudson's Bay store and she told me that she's coming here to see you today."

Anna jumped back under the quilt. Mommy Suzanne was coming! Hooray! And she was sober! Mommy Suzanne was real nice when she wasn't on the bottle. She had so many stories to tell and she always laughed a lot.

When Anna woke up, she could hear Mommy Suzanne and Ama laughing in the next room. She could smell caribou and barley soup cooking. Through the tiny window above the bed, she saw that it was getting dark outside. She got out of bed and went in the kitchen to smile shyly at her mother.

Black Marie was gone. Harry was standing in his playpen, rattling the bars and babbling, and Violette was home from school, sitting at the table with a piece of hot bannock and raspberry jam. Ama had turned the electric light on.

Mommy Suzanne kissed both Anna's cheeks, picked her up and gave her a big hug. "Oh, let me look at you! You're growing so big! Before we know it you'll be all grown-up! What grade are you in now? Grade five! Oh my Goodness! Here, you go sit with Ama and I'll get the soup finished for you kids."

Anna climbed onto Ama's lap, her gangly legs hanging down, and listened to the talk floating in the warm, food-scented air. Ama rubbed some Vicks VapoRub on Anna's chest and wrapped her in an oven-warmed towel as they listened to Mommy Suzanne's stories. "One time when I was working in Con Mines…Oh Ama, you would have laughed! The boss's wife, her name was Hilda. Hill-DAA! She had yellow, yellow hair like I'd never seen before in my life. Yes siree, piled all up on top of her head in big round curls, all sprayed stiff as cardboard with that Adorn hairspray, eh? And held together with a million bobby pins. When they started to slip, she looked like a little porcupine! But, oh Lord, in the morning when it was down hanging around her face. I'm telling you, she could scare a sled dog half to death! So anyway, I'm working there as a waitress, eh? So many, many years ago. You remember Con Mines, Anna? I took you there to sleep overnight when you were just a tyke.

"Anyways, Anna, you know me, I see everything. I see how the cook, he's just a little skinny little guy and he's always watching Hilda. She has eyes for him, too. I can tell by the way she walks past him. Like this." And Mommy Suzanne raised herself up on her tiptoes and minced over to Ama. She took Anna by the hand, they both stuck their noses in the air, and pranced to the table, giggling. Mommy Suzanne put Anna on the chair next to Violette and danced away, one hand on her hip, the other crooked at the elbow, waving the soup ladle. With her bum wiggling furiously and batting her stubby eyelashes, she dished out the soup. Anna and Violette laughed and laughed.

Ama mashed up the soup real good for Harry. She pinned a big tea towel around his neck and held him on her lap while she fed him.

Mommy Suzanne went on with her story while everyone ate. "Well. After awhile, the boss, George, his name was, he finally sees the big googly eyes going on between the cook and his wife, eh?

"So, the next day at suppertime, the big gas grill in the kitchen is going like crazy! All the miners are in for their dinner, and all the staff was running around in big circles. It was just nuts every day at dinner time, I'm telling you! The little cook was sweating away, so much water running down his face it was like a river.

"George the big boss, he comes in and he stands there for a minute in the corner like this." And Mommy Suzanne drew her short little self up tall. She puffed out her chest, tucked in her chin, stuck out her lip, and screwed up one eye. "He put his hands on his big fat hips." Mommy Suzanne put her hands on her hips and swung her chest from side to side. "He was just looking and looking at that cook flying around that big hot stove.

"And George, he was a big man, eh? Six foot tall at least. After awhile he comes over and he picks the cook up like this." Mommy Suzanne twisted her blouse all tight at her neck and stood up on her toes. She bugged her eyes out and made gagging noises. "Ach…ach. So, big George has the little cook by his skinny red chicken neck. He lifts him up, up, right off the floor. Ohmygod, you should have seen how purple that poor cook's face turned. And *then* George holds him right over that burning hot stove! Oh you should have seen it! His bum was only about an inch away from being fried real good. And his little legs were going, going like this." By now Mommy Suzanne was laughing so hard, she had to wipe her eyes with one hand while she held the other out and made her two front fingers run real fast.

Mommy Suzanne was laughing so hard, she began to choke.

"And that was the end of the big romance at Con Mines!"

Ama frowned most horribly and went "Heh, heh. What a story to tell in front of the little kiddies, Suzanne."

Anna, sensing the change in the room beginning, slid from her chair and tugged at Mommy Suzanne's pullover. "Mommy, are you a half-breed like me?"

Mommy Suzanne looked kind of funny for a split second. Then she laughed. "Yup, we are all half-breeds in this family, sweetie, except for your Ama. She's a full blood. Oh! And so is little Violette here and that fat new little brother you got. So cute. Little Eskimo pie!

"But anyways, your daddy, Anna, he was half-breed too. Ooh, he was a handsome devil! Part French and part Cree from northern Alberta. Just you listen to what your grandma's name was! That was your daddy's mother, eh? Her name was so pretty! Louise De LaBouton De Rose. It means little rose button. Can you imagine that!

"And me, I'm part Russian to hear your old Grandpa Ernie tell it. And the other half is Dogrib. What a combo, eh? That's for sure. And you, you're so lucky, on your dad's side, your great, great grandpa is old King Mercredi! He had so many wives, nobody could count them all! He was a French man. Oooooweeee gay Par-eee! Ha haaa!"

"*Suzanne!*" Ama looked in a real bad temper…"Stop telling the kid such nonsense. I never heard such big lies in all my life!"

"Oh Ama, you know it's the truth. What's to be ashamed of there? Your old Ama, Anna, she don't like people having a good time." Mommy Suzanne winked at the little girls.

"*Suzanne!*"

Ama grumbled when Mommy Suzanne talked to Anna too much, but she sure seemed happy to have her around most of the time. Mommy Suzanne scrubbed and waxed the floors. She helped with Harry. She dragged out the wringer washing machine and did the clothes, hanging them outside on the line to dry. When she brought them in, the clothes were frozen stiff as boards. That was fun. Ama and Mommy Suzanne would string up clothes lines all over the kitchen and cover the floor with newspaper to catch the melt. Then they would stuff lots of wood in the fire. The little house would be hot and steamy, smelling of fresh ice water. "Good for the whooping cough, eh Ama?" laughed Mommy Suzanne.

She was a real good cook. Mommy Suzanne could make pork chops with pineapple and bake cakes to eat with canned apricots. She could make icing out of coconut and brown sugar and cut the caribou for dry meat. She could roast a muskrat tail just right over the fire. She was generous and bought lots of food, even the good instant mashed potatoes, and the peanut butter with jam swirled through it like a candy cane. She sang funny songs while she worked. It's been a blue, blue day. I feel like running away. I feel like running away from the bloo-oohs. She and Ama would talk for hours. The days passed quickly.

"Yessiree, I can act just as stuck up as any white woman I tell you!"

"You think that's something to be proud of?" muttered Ama, bouncing Harry on her knee and casting a dark flash at Mommy Suzanne.

Mommy Suzanne flashed right back and went on gaily, "But that's not the life for me. Fiddle dee dee! Hey, Ama, did I tell you about the trip to Niagara Falls for the honeymoon with Tom?"

Ama looked full of wonder. "Honeymoon?"

"Honeymoon, I'm a singin' in June. Oh you should see the outside Ama! Full of cars. And the buildings are *so* tall! They have to have elevators in them. Little boxes that go up and down between the floors. They carry people so the people don't have to walk up the stairs. Lazy huh? Ten stories to those buildings at least. Some even higher. But the cars on the roads. They call them highways outside. Ooh, what a stink! You never smelled anything so bad in all your life, I'm telling you. Worse than rotten fish!" Mommy Suzanne pinched her nose and made a disgusted face. She kept on talking.

"And there's so many electric lights at night, there must be more than the stars in the sky. They can make you blind, they're so bright. You can't see anything else. It's just like daytime when all those lights are on." Mommy Suzanne squinted and blinked her eyes real fast. "Coloured lights too! Just like Christmas all year round. But not like here in the bush where we have the northern lights. Ahh. It's too pretty up here to leave for long.

"You wouldn't like it in the city Ama, it stinks, it's noisy, and there's so many people pushing you here and there on the sidewalk. People are real stuck up outside I tell you. And here in Yellowknife, we think that Mrs. DeCotret is stuck up! Did I tell you I heard in the bar that Mrs. DeCotret, she's part Indian herself? Yes-sireeee. From Quebec! Who would of thought it when she likes to act so white!"

Ama almost dropped Harry on the floor.

"NAWWWW! How could that be? You say Mrs. DeCo*Tret* is part Indian her own self? With the way she acts in this town Suzanne? Tsumah Tweh! What a big stinker! You know what she did to me just a while ago? Disclenyeh! Anna, she's so smart now, she's in that Mrs. DeCotret's class at the school eh? Anyways, that Mrs. DeCotret, she teaches the French to all the kids.

"Well, I know my French, that's for sure. I learned it real good in the convent. We couldn't talk nothing else in there. So

I'm helping Anna with her homework and the paper asks what the word for potato is eh? In French. It's pomme de terre I tell her. So the next day, poor little Anna, she comes back from school crying to beat the band. Mrs. DeCotret told her pomme de terre was wrong. And the correct word is patate. But Anna, she stood up for herself and she defended me, told Mrs. DeCotret that I spoke French perfect! So that stuck up thing, she goes to the priest. Can you figure that out? To the priest himself just to show what a big shot she is! She wants to make trouble for me. To show that she's better. She tells the priest I'm teaching my own kid the wrong thing and interfering with her lessons at the school. She says the right word is patate. From Quebec! Well. I was forced to go to school with those Grey Nuns from Quebec. And they are the same ones who taught me to say pommes de terre. Apples of the ground."

Mommy Suzanne was proud of Anna. "So. My little girl is a toughie! She looks as sexy as Marilyn Monroe already and she's as smart as anything too!"

"*Suzanne! Bonne Dieu!* The things you say in front of such innocent little kids. Watch your dirty mouth! What a nerve! Using those words in this house! Must be one of those fancy ideas you picked up in the bar. The way you drink my girl, I hear all about you. You think I'm just an old woman that doesn't know nothing but I'm smarter than you think. And I say to shut your filthy mouth in front of my kids Suzanne, tsk!"

"What are you talking about, Ama? Your kids? Who do you think Anna's real mother is?" Mommy Suzanne saw Ama's pale face. She stopped for a minute, but she couldn't help herself and kept on. "Did you see me take a drink in the past few days? Did you? I told you I quit. Why don't you ever take my word for anything? Why do you always believe the worst? Why are you so hard-hearted?"

Ama put on her stubborn face. "You're the one made me hard-hearted. Sure you can go without for a few days. I've seen that before. But who knows when you'll start again. I've heard your lies too many times already."

"Awwww Ama, we were having such a good time, why do you want to start again, eh? Maybe it's you that wants to drive me back to the bottle with all your whining." Ama and Mommy Suzannne started talking in Dogrib. They had a long fight. It lasted until bedtime.

The next morning, Mommy Suzanne had to go to see the RCMP. She put on her real tight red banlon sweater and her even tighter black stretchy ski pants. She wore high heels and lipstick. She spit into the little red plastic box of mascara and rubbed the teeny toothbrush in it. The she brushed her eyelashes into stubby stiff spikes and sang "May-bell-ine, why can'tcha be troo-ooooh." And laughed and talked in Dogrib to Ama who was changing Harry's diaper. Ama still looked mad.

Anna knew in her bones that Mommy Suzanne was leaving again. She sidled up to her mother and slid her arms around Mommy Suzanne's waist.

"How come you have to go see the police Mommy? Aren't you scared to go to the police station?"

Mommy Suzanne just laughed and smoothed her hands all up and down her sweater and over her hips. "Nah, Anna, don't worry, it's nothing. Just a little accident while I was in Fort Smith. Anyways, chin up! Those police will be nice to me when they see this, isn't that right, Ama?"

Ama gave Mommy Suzanne a real dirty look. "Ayeeeeesh!

You're so hurtful! Just like a knife in my heart. And what a thing to say in front of a Anna. Shut your dirty mouth in front of her, Suzanne."

"Oh for Pete's sake, why? Look at her. She's growing up and she'll know soon enough eh? Yes sir, RCMP or no RCMP. A man is always the same when he pulls his pants down! You remember that Anna!" She laughed some more. "Yessireeee, those police will be nice when they see this alright, their big eyes will be bugging out and they'll forget what I went there for in the first place. O-KAYYYY, Suzanne, they'll say. Cheer-i-oh! They'll say. Come back real soon now you hear! Cheerio!" Mommy Suzanne laughed so hard she had to hang onto the washstand with one hand. The glint of teardrops squeezed out between her short little eyelashes. Big black smudges smeared under her eyes.

Ama didn't care at all about those teardrops. "Hmmph! Cheerio alright! Just so long as you don't stop at no darn bar on the way back home." She swished huffily into the bedroom with Harry held in front of her like a battle shield.

Mommy Suzanne took the washcloth and wiped the mascara from under her eyes. She rinsed the cloth in the basin and hung it on the hook above the washstand. Then she put on put on her parka and her boots. She stopped and looked real serious at Anna standing miserably by the stove in her pajamas and red plaid slippers.

"Come my darling, come and give your old Mommy Suzanne a kiss for luck." Mommy dug around in her big black shiny plastic purse and found her smokes. She lit one up and crouched in front of Anna. "You listen to me good now, okay my little Eskimo pie? I don't think I'll be coming back for awhile. Your Ama and me, after awhile, we always seem to get on each other's nerves.

She was my Ama too, you know, when I was just a little girl like you. But sometimes, I don't know. Living with those damn nuns in a convent can drive you nuts. Ama was with the nuns too long. She prays too much and I've heard she sees things now, too. Is that true?"

Anna felt embarrassed. She looked at her feet. Last year, on Good Friday, Ama had seen God. "Oh my! Oh my dear Lord!" Ama had knelt down right in the middle of the road. Right in front of the house where Anna and Violette had been playing hopscotch. "Kneel down with me, my girls." And Ama had pulled their sleeves until they knelt down beside her. "Do you see? There in the sun! Hah? What's that in the sun Anna? Violette? It's like a crucifix there, I tell you."

Anna and Violette stared. They looked at each other and back at Ama. Ama had tears coming from her squeezed tight eyes. Her lips were moving in prayer. The sun shone on her little moustache.

Anna couldn't tell on her Ama. No matter what.

Mommy Suzanne sighed. "Well, never mind, then. I can tell you're not going to say anything about the old bat. But, you know I'm your real mother, don't you?"

Anna nodded. She felt pretty awful, and she wasn't sure why.

She felt bad over Mommy Suzanne talking about Ama. And she felt bad about Mommy Suzanne going away and leaving her again.

"Hey, look at me now. I have something real important to tell you, okay? It doesn't matter really if you're Indian or White or Métis, okay? It doesn't matter if you're Chinese. Doesn't matter what the God damn colour of anyone's skin is, okay? As long as people are decent to each other, nothing else matters. There's good white people around, and there's bad Indians too. You take each person as they come, and don't let any one take advantage of you. If any one hurts you, you give them the old WHUMPF! Frozen mukluk in the balls! Yessirr. You have to be tough to grow up in this world Anna, I'm not funnin' you. I don't want you to grow up with hate in your heart and being afraid of people because of the colour of their skin or the way they talk or how much money they say they have. You don't be scared of no one and be proud of yourself. Just hold your head right up there, okay? Promise me?"

"Sure Mommy. Good luck. I love you Mommy. Bye."

BROOM Story

It was summer. Baby Harry's parents had come back from hunting on the barren lands. The welfare worker had driven up in her big sparkly car with the flaring fins and taken him away. Ama was moping around inside the house.

Violette and Anna were playing on the swing in the front yard. They were fooling around, taking turns. One would lie across the wooden seat on her stomach while the other twisted the swing round and round until the rope was so tight it couldn't twist any more. Then whoever was twisting would let go and jump out of the way. The swing would go flying round and round really fast. Anna staggered off the swing, holding her stomach. "Whoa! Ever good that time! I think I'm gonna throw up!"

Violette began swinging on the gate, looking dreamily down the road. "Hey Anna, look! Your Mommy Suzanne's coming."

Anna lurched over to the fence. "Huh? That's not her. I don't even think she's in town. Maybe it's somebody else."

The two girls went to the corner of the front yard and hung over the fence to get a better look.

Violette looked at Anna. "That sure looks like your Mommy Suzanne to me."

"Gee. You're right. I didn't even know she was in town. I wonder what she's done with Tina and Tommy this time."

Anna knew something bad had happened to her Mommy Suzanne and Loulou and Mickey were gone. Their daddy had taken them far away and they were never coming back. Now Mommy Suzanne and Tina and Tommy moved around a lot. Sometimes the welfare took Tina and Tommy away and put them in foster homes or residential schools. Sometimes they were with Mommy Suzanne. Ama complained about it a lot.

Anna squinted her eyes and peered just as hard as she could. "It *is* Mommy Suzanne! Wowee, just look at her!"

Mommy Suzanne was getting closer. Her face looked kind of funny. Her eyes were all red and weird and her mouth was hanging open all loose. Anna crouched behind the wild rose bushes that lined the front fence, pulling Violette down with her. They hid in the clean fresh perfume, watching through the little sawtoothed leaves and velvet pink petals.

Mommy Suzanne's hair was coming undone from its bun. Her blouse was all untucked from her tight black ski-pants. She had no socks on. Her ankles looked white and scaly and her sneakers were really grimy and had no shoelaces so they flapped in the dust like bedroom slippers.

"She looks really drunk, eh? Let's go hide better!" Violette hissed, tugging Anna away from the fence and the wild roses.

Mommy Suzanne was almost in front of them, she had reached the fence.

They ran around the corner of the wooden six-sided warehouse where Ama kept boxes of camping equipment, tools, traps, old clothes, pots, pans, and a fascinating gold and white striped box of Max Factor's Hollywood make-up. Peeping around the corner, they watched Mommy Suzanne wobble through the gate, weave down the front path and disappear inside the house.

Anna and Violette went to sit on the steps of the clothes platform and talk. "She's allays drunk eh?" whispered Violette, looking scared.

Anna gave Violette a sisterly little shove. "Awww, c'mon ya little dummy, you're too small to know what's drunk. *Drunk.* Drunk-drunk-drunk!"

Violette shoved back. "Am not! And anyways, I was closer than you and I saw her crying."

"Huh?...Nahhhh. Betcha she's just drunk. C'mon, let's go-see."

Creeping, giggling, choking. "Shhhhhhh!" Tripping. Two pairs of goggling brown eyes around the corner of the door frame.

The house looked strange. So dark it blurred Anna's and Violette's eyes after the bright, sun-drenched afternoon. Blood red dots danced before them in the grey shadows.

Violette hissing in the cool dark. "Go in! Gwan, she's *your* Mommy Suzanne...I'll just wait here for you, okay? C'mon, sssssss! C'mon! You scared?"

"NO! Course not! You first! Hey! Leggo! C'mon leggo."

"Y'are too scared! Scared cause she's crying."

"She's always crying when she's drunk."

"So? C'mon then!"

Then Ama's long pale pinched face all of a sudden from out of the dusky quiet. Ama's mouth all tight. Ama's arms holding Mommy Suzanne.

Shhh Shhhhhhhhhh. Rocking her back and forth like a little baby.

"Ssshhhh my girl. Shh...the kids are looking. Shh now, shhh, husha husha." Ama looked up at Anna and Violette. "You kids go on outside to play now. Go on! There's nothing for you in here now. Go away to play for awhile now. *Go!*"

They went away to the clothesline. Sitting on the silvered wooden steps of the clothes platform. Anna played her plastic guitar.

Violette caught the really big ants and pulled the legs off, one by one. They sang together. "Hang down yer head *Tawm* doo-oooh-leee!!! Hang down yer head an' cry-yyy. Hang down your heh."

Violette held up an especially fat long ant. A good one. "*Here*! Here's a nice big one! You do it this time. *C'mon* just pull'em off! *Yeah*! Pull them one at a time. *See! See!* Now he walks like he's drunk...eh?"

"ANNN...AHHHHH...Anna! ANN-AHHH! COME! Come in here now! Violette! Veeee-oh-lette! An-ahhhhh!"

Violette dropped the last ant to stagger drunkenly over the great cliff of the step. Anna flung her guitar to the top of the platform for safekeeping. Tripping over one another's feet to get to the house. Ama pulling them inside and looking around just in case any nosy neighbours were watching.

"Violette you run...run to the, no. No. Wait. I have to go

telephone now. Right now and you take this broom oh my God and you go you listen good now my poor girls. You go help that Mommy Suzanne go sweep the floor around her till I get back Violette you hold the dustpan help your sister. Now go oh my God go fast I'm telling you." Ama took off her apron and rushed out the door. She didn't even stop to take her purse or put on her kerchief.

Anna grabbed the broom from the porch and ran into the bedroom. Violette was right behind.

Frozen quiet. In the doorway. Stopped by the chair in the middle of the room. The chair standing alone in the middle of the room like a tiny wooden island with a giant humpbacked Mommy Suzanne all crouched over on it. Mommy Suzanne whimpering and trying to climb up the back of the little blue chair.

"Oh-my-God." Mommy Suzanne holding her knees to her chest. "God-oh-God." Holding her bare and dirty feet, her toes all spread apart and curled up stiff. "They're coming Annnn-ahhhh!" Pulling on her mouth. Spit slimy wet all over. "Anna-oh-sweep-for me-oh." Tears all over Mommy Suzanne's face, dripping from her chin. Her hair all wet and stuck in clumps to her cheek. "Sweep-away-the-buggers." Pulling her eyes red inside. "Oh plee-eeese."

Crying. "Oh God! They're uh ahuh...*sweep* you little bastards, oh-my-God gogo faster aha a ha ha heh Aaaiieee they're climbing up the God damn *chair* oh take them away *pleee-ease* there! T*here!!* *Can't* you *see-eee.* There! *Oh God.* Damn *you!* You little *sluts!* Oh Jesus *God*! *Fuh-fuh*king virgin! Hell-you-sweep!"

Anna and Violette, icy cold with fear, sweeping around and around the scary not-Mommy-Suzanne anymore perched on the small chair. Sweeping away clean pink roses printed on grey linoleum. Sweeping the sun from the floor. Sweeping away the devil snakes. Sweeping away mommy spiders.

Sweeping away the real bad words. Sweeping up all the bogeymen real fast.

Violette with the tea towel, wiping the invisible wet nothing off of the chair legs. Shit and. Blood and. Snakes and. Nothing. All over the clean, clean floor.

Dust motes dancing, sparkling golden in the sunbeams coming through the bedroom window.

Ama looked in the door. She was back from telephoning at the neighbours.

"Ama, there's nothing on the floor, honest."

"Shhhh, just sweep now my girls, the priest, he's coming. Sweep now for your Mommy Suzanne."

"But Ama..." Trying to be brave but crying all the same.

Violette crying too, little rivers running down over her fat funny round chin, following Anna with the dust pan.

Ama took out her rosary and knelt down on the floor. "Kneel down and pray with me now, my girls. Holy Mary, Mother of God, pray for us now and at the hour of our death."

Mommy Suzanne howling and muttering, pulling her lips, scratching her face and bleeding on her chin. Scratching her face down hard, all crazy wet, squealing, then whispering and looking all around like a crazy woman, then all of a sudden waving her arms and yelling..."Aa-iiii...Oh-I-can't! I *can't*. *Oh!* Oh.

"Get. Away! Snaaaa-yaaaa-ssssss sssssnakes!!! *Snake*. Ohhhhhhh Gaaaw. *Fu*cking *goddamn*. They-re pulll-ing me...*Help me*."

Ama reaching out to pat Mommy Suzanne and crooning in between Mommy's scary noises. "Shhhh now. Now, now Suzanne. Pull yourself together. Nothing can hurt you while the kids are here you know that. You know that eh, my girl? God is with them I tell you. Shhhhh now. No snakes can come around with the little innocents here beside you. There's nothing here to hurt you now. Shh."

Anna and Violette. "Hail Mary pray for us sinners now and at the hour of our death."

After forever the priest came, his robes swishing. He was muttering his prayers and sprinkling holy water before him as he came. Anna and Violette ran away to the clothes platform with all the doors shut tight behind them. Away to hold each other and try to stop their crying and fright and wait. Waiting for Ama to come out and the devils and snakes and bad, bad things to go away. Waiting for the priest to come out, talking low to Ama.

Waiting for Mommy Suzanne to go to sleep.

The **DEVIL'S** Work

Ama was in the bedroom sewing. She liked it there because she could spread all her sewing supplies out around her on the big double bed. All the moose hide pieces of the moccasins she was working on. The red zig-zag edged felt she used for trim, the rainbows of soft silk thread for embroidering leaves and flowers on the toes, bits of pulled taffy babiche to sew all the pieces together, and her black felt embroidered sewing bag with all its different pockets for needles, thimbles, and scissors. Violette was off playing somewhere outside. Anna was alone in the front room. She had dragged Ama's red plastic stuffed chair with the chrome legs from its usual spot by the wood stove to the washstand, and was kneeling on it, looking at herself in the mirror.

She heard rustling, then the squeak of the bedsprings. Ama came into the room. "Oh my God, looking in the mirror again.

Don't look in the mirror like that. What are you looking in there for anyways, hmm?"

"Nothing, Ama."

"Get down then." Ama took the chair, putting it back by the stove. Anna watched her sit down. Ama put one hand on each knee and looked at her daughter. "You're just a baby yet my girl, too young to be in front of the looking glass all the time." Anna came over to the comfort of Ama, but somewhat defiantly.

"I'm twelve years old now Ama, and the other kids at school make fun of me. They say I have big fat balloon lips."

"Who says that?"

"Foo Foo and her cousin from the flats. You know, Mary Pauline."

"They have a nerve talking to you like that. That one girl from the flats looks just like a little frog with her big bug eyes sticking out. And with the family that Foo Foo has, she has no right to be so stuck up herself. What a world! Pay no attention to them my girl. Come." Ama reached out her arm to Anna's hips and drew her closer.

Anna sat on the floor by Ama's beaded moccasins, put her arms around Ama's legs and rested her head on Ama's lap. Ama smoothed Anna's hair. "I'll tell you a story, my girl. Let me see now, it was your great great grand auntie. Her name was Suzanne, just like your mother. Yep, oh, she thought she was something, let me tell you. Always looking at herself. Everywhere! Every chance she got, she took it! Vain. It was the devil's work, I'm telling you. She was always looking at herself. In the water barrel, in the dishes, in the lake when she was taking up the fishing nets. She had a little looking glass that she kept in her apron all the time, too. She didn't think anybody knew, but I was just a little girl then and I saw. It was just before that bad time when I went into the convent in Fort Resolution. I used to be such a nosy little girl, eh? And kids see everything all the time anyways. So, that Suzanne, she was always walking like this, hmph! And like that, hmph! She really thought she was something alright."

Anna looked up. "Was she pretty, Ama?"

"Hmph! Pretty! Everybody has a pretty face when they're young my girl. It's when we get old we turn ugly if we don't live right. Your great auntie, she shouldn't have been looking in that mirror all the time.

"So one time anyways, late, late at night when everyone was sleeping, I was sleeping too but I heard the story from one of the older girls later on. Suzanne was sitting all night on the floor by the fire. It was cold. She was looking at herself as usual. Turning this way, that way, just staring like she always did into that little looking glass she kept hidden in her pocket. And she could see the reflection of the fire in the mirror. She didn't feel so good watching that fire in the mirror though. She felt a little bit sick, her stomach seemed to be kind of upset, eh? It was turning around and around, over and over.

"But she thought she was just tired from staying up so late. Then the fire started going so funny. In the mirror her face was melting just like the wax of the candle, and she looked and looked. Oh yes, she stared and stared. She thought she was dead. Her heart stopped, she said. She saw the fire all around and she saw herself in the mirror. She saw herself in the grave. She saw herself when she was dead, I tell you. And something was whispering, whispering, it sounded kind of like the wood burning very low. It was going ssss in her ears. Very quiet, though, very soft, she could hardly hear it. Don't be so proud, the little black things were whispering, whispering to her, sitting there all alone in the middle of the night. She was cold. Cold like it was in the middle of winter, I tell you. And it was only March.

"The little fire in the wood stove, it was hissing like little devil snakes. But great great grand auntie, she could see no snakes, no matter how hard she looked in all the corners of the room. All she could see was the fire in the looking glass, and her face staring back at her. Dead. Someday you'll look just like this, those little voices were hissing, hissing. She couldn't look. She closed her eyes. And still, she could hear that little, little sssss. Don't be so proud my friend. Little little snakes in her ears wouldn't stop. Saying, yes, yes when you are dead you won't be so good looking. Yes, and what will be left to be so proud of then, hmm? Your looks will die too, eh?

"And Suzanne, she opened her eyes, wide, wide, wide. And she took a real good look. And she threw that little mirror in the fire. BANG it went." Ama clapped her hands together loud by Anna's ear. Anna jumped. Ama went on. "And after that time, oh! She didn't walk like this, hmph! And like that hmph! And she didn't turn her head this way and that way with her nose stuck up in the air anymore. She didn't pretend to be better than other people for no good reason. No. She became so good-hearted! If anyone needed something…'Here,' she said, 'Here. Take it!' And from that day on, the very next morning, I tell you, she always had a big, good-hearted smile for everyone and she took care of her kids. Oh! She could do anything. Fishing, trapping and nice, nice beadwork. Oh, she could sew fine, fine stitches. Everybody was so jealous of her moccasins and mukluks. But she was never mean to anyone. Now that was sure something to be proud of. She never looked down her nose at anyone again.

Hey…She was a good woman then. So my girl, you always do your best for your people. That is what there is to be proud of. Never look down your nose at anyone and think to yourself that you are better than they are. That is the devil's work."

LEMON Tree

It was the first of July. Ama loved holidays and tried her best to buy the kids new clothes for as many of them as she could afford at the time. This bright summer morning, they were decked out as fine as they ever were. Both Anna and Violette wore brand new snowy white running shoes, the fresh rubber and canvas smell promising a summer vacation of adventures and fun. They wore matching, above-the-knee, crisp and never-washed, sky-blue pedal pushers. "The colour of the Virgin Mary!" Ama announced proudly to the clerk in the Weaver and Devore store while Anna rolled her eyes in embarrassment and Violette watched Anna closely. Both girls sported pale blue striped seersucker tops with a fuzzy white fringe around the belly button. Best of all, they wore the very latest fashion in Yellowknife: neon bright socks. Anna wore screeching pink and Violette had Kool-Aid lime green.

The first of July celebration in Yellowknife, Northwest Territories, took place at ten a.m. sharp at the Gerry Murphy Arena beside the Stanton Hospital on Frame Lake.

Ama, Anna, Violette, and Black Marie were waiting at the bus stop promptly at 9:20 a.m. so they could catch the first bus uptown at 9:30. The girls were beside themselves with excitement. Ama and Black Marie were wearing their best dark blue skirts and flowered kerchiefs. They each had a shopping bag with a blanket and sweaters in case it turned cool. "You guys get dirty and we're going straight home! You hear me?"

"You get out of that dirt right now! Anna! Violette! You're too big to be playing in the dirt like that! Stop hanging backwards on the swing like that! Your hair is dragging in the sand. What's wrong with you two little devils this morning anyways?" Black Marie and Ama were both sweating and out of temper by the time the old yellow school bus drew up in a cloud of choking dust.

The girls bounced aboard, bounced to the back of the bus, and bounced on their squeaky leatherette seats all the way to the arena. Ama and Marie sat in the very front seat behind the driver, as far away as they could get from the giggling noisy devils that had lost their minds.

When the bus dropped them off in front of the hospital, oh! What a day it was! There wasn't a cloud in the new blue sky. The waves on Frame Lake sparkled through the fresh green leaves of the bushes growing on the shore. The sun shone warmly, banishing all memory of the winter past, of forty below snow banks and whiteouts. A little breeze blew off the lake, and the whole town seemed to be smiling in the small park sandwiched between the arena and the hospital.

There were parades, starting with toddlers on tricycles festooned with crêpe paper, streamers, balloons, and blowsy roses made out of pastel coloured toilet paper and bobby pins. Then a fewer older children followed on two-wheeled bikes, decorated somewhat more sparsely. They were followed by an important and boring parade of the Grand Order of Elks, a few old men with what seemed to be upside-down purple sand buckets with cheesy gold tassels springing out of the centre on their heads. They marched very slowly and solemnly, knees up, their eyes straight ahead and their arms swinging high. The loudspeaker from the arena squealed out a tinny, faint, "Oh Canada."

Black Marie pointed and hissed at the girls. "Those old white guys won't put on the celebration next year unless you clap real loud!" She put on her especially fake grin and clapped loudly. Ama stood at attention beside Black Marie, clapping like a proper lady. She held one hand out, stiffly bent at the elbow. With her free hand, she slapped the stationary hand as loud as she could. Anna and Violette clapped until their hands turned red and stung.

Then the fun began.

Ama and Black Marie split up during the course of the long day, each finding old friends they hadn't seen for a long time. Most of the old people sat in small groups under the shade of the trees in the park. The old aunties pulled their kerchiefs down around their hot talcum-powdered necks. They kicked off their rubbers and sat, moccasined feet and tan-stockinged legs straight out in front of them. They fanned themselves with whatever they could lay their hands on. A few of them smoked their pipes. The men squatted nearby or leaned against the trees. Children ran in and out of the arena, according to what was going on at the time.

In the busy, sun-melted morning, there were three-legged

races, potato sack races, wheelbarrow races and relays for all ages. There were just plain old all-out races for each age group. The prizes were stiff shiny buttons that looked like flowers. They were made out of satin, had a pin on the back, and two ribbons hanging down. Purple was first prize, yellow second, and white third.

After this, in the arena, there were steamed hotdogs, pink prickly clouds of cotton candy, wieners dipped in batter and deep-fried crispy on a stick, potato chips, french fries, soft ice cream in a cone, kewpie dolls on a stick, go fish, roulette wheels, throw-a-dart-at-a-balloon-and-win-a-stuffed-tiger, and best of all in Anna's eyes, prizes of impossible-to-win ceramic shining black panther lamps luring fools to rush in and spend money at differently-named draws and bingos. Bingo was the only game that brought the old people into the arena and away from the shade of the trees for a few minutes.

In the late afternoon, all their money and energy spent, the girls dragged their weary feet out to search for Ama under one of the trees. Finally, they found her sitting down by the lake where it was coolest. They flopped on the blanket beside her. "We're so tired, Ama."

"What do you expect? You've been running around like two crazy things all day. You spent all the money, there's not even enough for bus fare."

"That's okay, Ama. We don't mind walking. You want to see what we got?" Anna dumped out her plastic loot bag onto the blanket. Ama looked at the trinkets. There was a genuine Wild West Indian head dress with brilliant green and yellow feathers, a plastic charm bracelet, and a small black ceramic statue of a growling panther.

"Good work," said Ama. "How about you Violette, my little girl." Violette shyly showed her Mickey Mouse balloon, her little Indian Princess headband with the gaudy coloured ostrich feather, and her five kewpie dolls won in go fish. "That's nice, that's real pretty. Are you happy now? You had a good time?" Violette nodded and Ama lit a cigarette. She looked at them. "You kids have been real busy bees for sure. But you have to walk home without me. I'm too tired to walk that far after waiting for you all day. And there's still some people I haven't seen in a long time here." Ama fished in her big black plastic handbag. "Here's the key for the padlock Anna. Take it and don't lose it now. I'll be home in a little while, okay? Okay. You go now, take Violette. You're a big girl now, you know how to make yourselves something to eat if you get hungry, eh? Don't worry, I'll be home in little while."

Violette fretted all the way home. She kept asking. "Where's Ama, Anna? How come she's not coming with us?"

"She told me she's coming after awhile, don't worry. I can take care of the both of us. Come on, it's not that far now. Let's race, okay? It'll go faster if we run."

"I can't run. I have a stitch."

The girls straggled down the mile long hill between the new town and the old town, dragging their ten-ton bags of prizes. Past the Peace River and Willow Flats, around the big rock where the Weaver and Devore store and the priest's house and the wharves for the big boats and the floatplanes were. They dragged their feet over the little gravel bridge between the rock and Latham Island, up the hill past the Indian Agents and Grandpa Harrison's and the Rex Café. Past the bus stop where they had bounced and giggled, waiting for the big yellow bus to take them to the first of July celebrations such a long, long day ago. Finally, in the cool of the seven o'clock evening, they were home. They had the hot, dusty feel of a long time away. A long time travelling.

Anna unlocked the padlock. They went inside the house. It seemed strange and very empty without Ama there to make a fire in the woodstove and cook dinner for them.

"It's just damp and chilly in here, that's all. Ama will be home soon," she said. They put some newspaper and kindling in the big woodstove and started a little fire. Anna warmed a can of baked beans while Violette took a tomato out of the little plastic train-shaped box in the new fridge. The rumbling Frigidaire was from the second hand store beside the Weaver and Devore Store and Ama had to sew and sell four pairs of mukluks to pay for it. Violette cut up the tomato while Anna buttered slices of bread. They turned on the radio and listened to it while they ate dinner. There was marching band music because it was the first of July. Anna boiled water in the kettle and poured it into the dishpan in the sink, along with a liberal squeeze of Lux detergent.

They didn't have running water and there were no faucets, but the drain worked. They could dump the water in the sink and it would rush out of the pipe in the back of the house. Anna washed and Violette dried. Together they put the bowls back in the big wooden cupboard that stood beside the sink. Then they went outside to sit on the blue rocks and wait for Ama. It began to get as dark as it gets in the land of the midnight sun. It looked like the sun was setting. It was ten o'clock at night. Anna was a little bit scared. Ama had left them alone before, but she had always been home for bedtime or she had sent someone to watch them.

"Violette, you put on your pajamas and go to bed, okay? I'll wait for Ama. She couldn't be too long now. She's never stayed out so late before."

"I'm scared, Anna." Violette began to chew on her fingernails.

"Shh. It's okay. It'll be all right. You just go inside and put on your pajamas. Go to sleep, okay? Tell you what. Let's all sleep together in Ama's big bed. You go to sleep first, then when Ama comes home, we'll both climb in with you, okay? It'll be fun."

They went inside. Violette brushed her teeth, put on her pajamas and climbed into the big bed. Anna tucked the blankets under her chin, kissed her goodnight, and went into the front room. She turned the radio low and sat by the window to wait for Ama. She was very tired. The radio kept playing the same song. Lemon tree, very pretty and the lemon flower is sweet, but the fruit of the poor lemon is impossible to eat. Finally, the radio went off the air all by itself. Anna kept sitting by the window, afraid, and singing the lemon tree song softly to keep herself awake. Violette appeared at her elbow.

"What are you doing? You should be asleep long ago!"

"I couldn't sleep Anna. Are you scared too?"

"No. It's okay. She's probably on her way home by now. It's so late. The bus must have stopped running and she has to walk so it will take a real long time. Here, sit by me. Aren't you cold? The fire's gone out. I'll bring the blanket in here for us."

Anna brought in the big flowered quilt from the bed. She wrapped it around herself and Violette. They sat on the little sofa in front of the window, chins resting on the sill, holding each other and singing the first two lines of the lemon tree song over and over again. It was an endless dream. It went on so long. They were sick with sleeplessness. A big fly circled round and round in a strange, other-worldly silence. Lemon tree, very pretty and the lemon flower is sweet. Anna's head was buzzing softly, she could see pretty little purple shadows blooming ever so slowly under Violette's deep, taffy-brown eyes. The sky grew lighter. In the very strangest way, it looked just the same as the day before when it was sunny and blue-skyed and the first of July. Except it wasn't. And Ama still wasn't home.

"Do you think she's dead?"

The girls looked at each other. Anna was the oldest. She had to look after Violette. She thought of Ama's words. "Keep your chin up, my girl."

She hugged her sister tight. "Don't worry Violette. As soon as the radio comes back on it'll be morning, and we'll go ask Grandpa Harrison for some help. He has a jeep and a telephone. He'll find Ama for sure!"

Wake up wake up you sleepy heads. Come on, get up, get out of bed. When the red red robin comes bob bob bobbin' along. The radio came on at six a.m. Violette got dressed and without breakfast, she and Anna set off to the other end of the small island where Grandpa Harrison lived in his turquoise wood frame two-storey house.

It was cool outside. Long blades of grass were bent over under the weight of morning dew. The sun hadn't risen high enough to begin steaming and warming the land.

When they got to Grandpa's house, the door was open. "You wait here, Violette, don't come inside till I say, okay?"

"Okay."

Anna creaked open the door. It was dark and cold inside. It smelled bad like people had been drinking all night. Grandpa was sitting on his chair by the table. His grizzled head had fallen down on his chest. He looked like he was asleep. There were glasses and bottles and booze spilt all over the place.

Ama was sprawled diagonally across the bed on top of the covers. Her clothes were all wrinkled and every which way. Her dress was unbuttoned and Anna could see her slip and undershirt. Even worse, her dress was pulled up and her bloomers were showing. Her moccasins were still tied snugly around her ankles. There was a man on the other side of Ama, asleep under the covers. Loud snoring filled the stinking air.

"Grandpa! Grandpa!"

Grandpa jumped awake, snorting. His eyes were all red and watery looking. He stood up and pulled his suspenders up over his shoulders. "Uhh, what are you doing here so early? Go outside and wait."

Anna went out. "Shh, it's okay. Ama must have been too tired to come home so she slept here at Grandpa's. She's going to get up now." They sat on the doorstep very close to one another, watching the silvery swell and ebb of the gentle waves in the morning lake across the road. They waited.

After a few minutes, Ama came stumbling out of Grandpa's house. Something was wrong with her. She was still drunk. She couldn't walk. She didn't talk, not even to say hello. Not even to say she was sorry. All she did was groan. She started to fall down. Anna rushed over to hold her up.

"Violette, help me. Get on the other side. No wait, I'll hold her in front. You go behind and hold her bum. We can do it, come on." The two girls helped their Ama home. Sometimes she fell, but between both of them pulling and pushing, they got her back on her feet and headed in the right direction.

All the way down the road, curtains parted and nosy eyes

followed their progress. In front of the LeMoine's house, Ama tried to lay down and sleep right in the middle of the road. Nasty Mr. LeMoine came out to laugh at them. "Sure looks like you girls have your hands full this morning, eh! Someone sure had a good time last night though!"

"Oh, don't ask if poor Ama is okay or anything like that. Don't ask if we need any help. Big fatso! Like he never got drunk in his own life, himself!" Anna grumbled and muttered under her breath as they struggled to get Ama back on the way home. Violette started crying. Anna tried to encourage her. "Stop crying. It doesn't help. You got to be tough."

Finally, they made it to the front door. Violette propped Ama against the side of the house while Anna undid the padlock. They took her inside. Then they unwrapped Ama's moccasins and put her to bed with all her clothes on.

Anna made some pancakes for breakfast. Then she and Violette had a nap.

A few days later, Ama got all dressed up and went to see the doctor. She said it was just a check-up because she was an old lady and old ladies had to see the doctor regular.

Just before school started that summer, Ama told them that she had to go outside to the Charles Camsell Hospital. "Just for a few days, my kids. It's nothing. Don't worry, the welfare will find someone to take good care of you and I'll be back before you know it."

That was when their lives changed.

Caribou QUEEN

Mommy Suzanne was back in town with big sister. Big brother had been taken away and put in the hostel in Fort Smith after Mommy Suzanne got so drunk she set the house on fire and someone died.

Anna and Violette were sitting at the table putting together fairies. The priest had brought by a big box of old clothes for them and at the bottom, they had found two kits. Inside were the hard grey wax figures of fairies, along with small tubes of glue, coloured sequins, bits of tulle, and little gold and silver beads. The girls were busy decorating the tiny figures and whispering. Ama was having a nap in the bedroom. She said she must be getting old because she was tired all the time now and didn't feel so good. Violette nudged her big sister and hissed. "Ama's up! Go ask her now before she goes back to sleep again!"

Anna looked over her shoulder. Ama had appeared in her usual place by the stove. Anna brought the little fairy over to her. "Look Ama, pretty, huh?" Ama nodded. "I was thinking, Ama, I could bring it over to Mommy Suzanne's place and show it to Tina when I'm finished. I know where they live."

Ama swore." Disclenyeh!" She stared hard and sad at Anna, a bitter sour look around her mouth.

Violette looked up. She slid softly from her chair, leaving the fairy behind on the table. She went outside, closing the door quietly behind her. Ama started again.

"Why? Why I'm asking the good Lord, why, do you give me so much trouble? You're going to turn out just the same as Suzanne if you don't watch out. It's that devil's blood in you for sure! Why do you want to go see them anyways, eh? It's raining too. No I say. No. No you can't go see her."

"But Ama, she's my mom too. Anyways, it stopped raining while you were in the other room and I don't think Mommy Suzanne's so bad as people say. She's just down the road by the bus stop. It's not that far."

"Ay-eesh, you think you're so grown up. A thirteen-year-old, walking around the island by yourself. And you don't understand nothing yet about Suzanne and her boozing, you hear me? You think I tell you everything I hear?"

Ama's nose got all pinched up and white. She pulled her old wine-coloured sweater tight across herself and hunched her shoulders up in curling storm clouds of Players cigarette smoke. Unfiltered.

"I want to go see Tina, Ama…if Mommy's drunk, I won't even talk to her, I promise. Gee whiz, you don't know that she drinks every night. How could Tina go to school if Mommy

Suzanne drank every night? You were listening too much to Black Marie yesterday, that's all! Please Ama, I haven't seen them for so long."

"Just stop now! I've had enough of you. My God, I should be having a rest now that I'm so old and tired. You know I feel sick these days! You should be taking care of your old Ama instead of giving me such a bad time. Oh, the trouble I have. Go outside and get Violette, I want you to wash the floor now instead of talking nonsense to me. Go away now. I don't even want to look at you!" Ama stood up. She stomped into the bedroom with her cigarette and her ashtray. Anna stomped out to the front yard, slamming the door just a little behind her. Ama was sick, but she sure had a quick temper and Anna didn't want to get hit.

Violette was sitting on Ama's old blue rocks. "Is she going to let you go?"

Anna was furious. She glared at Violette, tears beginning to form in the corners of her eyes. "No! The old witch. I wish she was dead!"

Violette's eyes bugged out. She got a tiny mischievous grin at one side of her mouth. "Oh! You're bad, you're going to go to hell, you know, for talking like that!"

"I don't care!" Anna snuffled and thumped herself down on the rock beside Violette. "She's just an old hypocrite anyways. Remember how much she used to drink herself before she started feeling so old? Remember when we used to wake up in the morning all the time and old Timmy Blanchette and old Rose would be passed out on the floor? And old Timmy would be grinding his teeth?"

Violette started to laugh. "Remember at midnight mass? Everybody was singing and the church was all decorated with poinsettias. The big manger was up with the holy virgin Mary and baby Jesus. We were all dressed up in our new coats and all of a sudden. *Thump!* Old Timmy falls out of his pew, right into the middle of the aisle and starts grinding his teeth. All through the rest of the mass, grrrr! Grr! That was so funny!"

Anna stopped crying. "Yeah. But Ama is still a hypocrite. Always making us pray and pretending she's so holy to the priests and the nuns and all the neighbours. Then she would take us off to some old man's house and we'd have to stay there all night while they got drunk together."

Violette was still laughing. "Anna! You're really going to hell now! I can see the devil sitting right behind you, listening with his big pointed hairy ears! Remember how we had to sleep at the foot of the bed at Grandpa Roald's? And we'd wake up with their big stinky feet in our faces? And remember the time we were here at home and the Blanchette's came over to drink? And we snuck in the house and stole all their booze. Remember? We were trying to be so quiet, sneaking out, and all the bottles started clinking away."

Anna started snickering. "It was *your* fault!" She gave Violette a friendly push. "You were giggling away like always, and every time I looked at you, I'd start too!"

"No. It's you who always starts laughing." Violette shoved back. Anna put her arm around her sister. They grinned at each other. Violette went on with her story. "You were going to hide the booze in the dog house and they heard us and chased us outside but they were so drunk, they kept falling down. We were all running around in circles in the front yard."

The two girls went off into gales of laughter. Finally, they stopped and went into the house to wash the kitchen floor. They were sitting on the doorstep waiting for the floor to dry when Ama came out of the bedroom and sat by the stove again.

Anna went over to Ama and put her arms around the old lady's shoulders. "Are you feeling better now, Ama?"

"Yes, my girls. I'm sorry I lost my temper, but I worry so much about you Anna. Your Mommy Suzanne has changed for the worse in the past few years you know. I heard how she was dancing in the hotel, dancing on the table with no panties on, laughing her head off and calling herself the Caribou Queen. She's gone right to the dogs now." Ama got up and took the poker to stir up the fire. She sat back down, lit another cigarette and looked at the fire.

Anna was quiet, turning Ama's sky blue cigarette package over and over in her hands. Looking and not looking at the sailor with his beard in the corner. She didn't believe that about Mommy Suzanne. Dancing on the table maybe, but not the other stuff about the panties. Probably some dirty old mind had made it up.

Violette was back at the table, mumbling to herself, as she tried to glue the fiddly little fairy wings to the back of the doll.

"Mommy Suzanne sure was nice when she wasn't drinking though, eh Ama?"

"Oh, sure...sure she's as sweet as pie when she's sober. Hey I hate that bottle! It's been a long time she's been on that damn bottle. She doesn't even have her own kids anymore. Tina's the only one left with her and she's only fifteen years old. What kind of life is that for a young girl, with a drunk for a mother?"

"But Tommy's okay now, eh Ama? He's in the hostel in Fort Smith I heard. You think he likes it?"

"How would I know that, my girl? All I know is those

residential schools, they call them hostels now but it's the same thing. They're full of Indian and half-breed kids they take away from their parents because they say it's the law to go to school. Then those poor kids go home for the summer and half the time they forgot how to talk to their own parents! They look down their noses at their own blood. Their skin is still brown but they think like white people. What a life. But with a mother like Suzanne, heyyy, it's probably for the best that Tommy's in there.

"What a mess. What a big mess! And that poor Tom. I didn't used to like him when Suzanne married him at first. I thought he was too hard on her. But that man, he sure put up with a lot from Suzanne, with all her drinking and running around. She treated him like dirt I hear. Still, I wish he didn't take Loulou and Mickey to live with his old white mother. I'll never see them again until the day I die. Yes, the only way I'll see those two little angels again is when we're all in heaven, I tell you."

"Tina must be real lonesome, eh Ama? If Mommy Suzanne is drinking so much, she must be scared. Maybe you should go see if she's all right."

Violette looked up from where she was dancing her fairy on the edge of the table. She knew what Anna was doing.

Ama sighed. "Eh? No, I don't want to take the chance of running into Suzanne if she's drinking."

"But it's only two o'clock Ama, she couldn't be too drunk yet. And if she is drinking, it would be better to go get Tina away from her before it gets too late. What do you think?"

"Aiiee, nothing but worries! But I guess you're right. Okay, you go then if you have to! I'm too tired. But go right away, if that Suzanne is drinking, you tell Tina she has to come here for the night. That's the only reason I'm letting you go. Be sure to bring her straight here if there's any funny stuff going on. Tell her she can go home in the morning, eh?"

"Okay, I promise Ama. Bye! Bye, Violette!"

Off to see Mommy and Tina, skipping down the dirt road, heart full of anticipation.

Knock knock on the door.

Round brown moon face. One eye just a little bigger than the other. Something gold, shiny, wild, green and moony in the eye. The too big front teeth and the big brown flecked eye and the round brown forever-child face.

Anna's sister Tina.

"Heyy, Anna! Oh it's so good to see you! Ohh, I'm glad you came to visit. I haven't seen you for so long! Look at how big you are! Come in, come in. Mommy's not here now but we'll have a good visit, okay? Just you and me."

The clean, clean kitchen and the scrubbed enamelled woodstove and the hot smell of fire and Sunlight bar soap. The floor just washed, the News of the North spread out over the damp linoleum. And the oil cloth on the table gleaming, shining brown and green glass bottles standing in a row on tiny printed sprigs of three cherries to a bunch.

"Holy smokes Tina, is Mommy having a party tonight? What's all those bottles for?"

"We're not having a party, you big silly! This is Mommy's bar. This one's Lemon Gin. You want a little drink?"

"Huh? No way. We're too little. You know that!"

"Awww c'mon! There's nobody here but us. No one will ever know. I had a few drinks once and Mommy never found out. You mean you never even tasted booze yet? Come, sit down at the table with me and tell me how you're doing."

They sat down at the little table facing the window. Anna could see the new playground and the school bus stop across the street. She turned to her sister.

"Sure, I had a drink once. A few summers ago, Ama took us to Fort Resolution for a holiday, eh? Me and Violette and Harry. It was just before welfare took him away cause they found his mom. He was four and Ama was so proud of him she bought him a brand new turquoise baseball cap for the trip. It had white elastic to keep it on his head. And when we got there, me and Violette were teasing him and holding him over the hole in the outhouse and his hat fell down. Boy, was Ama ever mad at us!"

"Ha ha haaa ha ha! So you had a drink because his hat fell down the toilet? Haw haaw!"

"Don't be silly. I just forgot what I was telling you. Anyways, there was lots of aunties and uncles there, eh? And we all went together in canoes to camp on the Little Buffalo River. Ama showed us the house she was born in. It was really nice, Tina, you should have seen it! Two stories and all made of logs. There were no other houses around at all, and you could see the river from the house. I would sure like to live in a house like that. Ama said her dad built it before he died."

"I don't want to hear about Ama's old house out in the bush! Tell me about you."

"Well, we all pitched tents on the other side of the river and had supper. They had a whole bunch of home brew, and they put us kids to bed so they could drink. We had a mosquito net in our tent! The sky was all pink and purple like Easter eggs outside when the sun was setting. Was it ever pretty! Violette and Harry fell asleep, but I couldn't sleep so I went outside to see what the grown-ups were doing and they had a big fire going and they were all sitting around and singing...I remem-berr the night of the Tenn-eseee waltz. One uncle gave me a penny and I gave it back to him for a glass of home brew. And then he gave me a penny change so I could buy another glass. Everybody was laughing and laughing at me. Even Ama! After awhile somebody started playing the fiddle. The moon came up so big and yellow that night Tina, it just about filled the whole sky. And then, I don't remember nothing else. I just woke up in the tent in the morning. We went back to Fort Resolution that day. It sure was a good summer. I wish we could go back sometime. I wish I could travel around with you and Mommy Suzanne, you've been everywhere, huh? You ever been to Fort Resolution with Mommy, Tina?"

Tina got up from the table. "No, I don't think so." She took two glasses from the cupboard and poured one half full of Lemon gin. She sat back down. Her eye got a little bigger and she grinned at her little sister before taking a sip. "Ahh," she said "that hits the spot." Anna giggled.

Tina took a bigger drink.

"You sure you don't want to try a sip? It won't kill you, you know. Here, taste this. It doesn't taste like booze. Goes down real nice and smooth." Tina smacked her lips and held out the glass, shaking it at Anna.

And Anna, who wanted desperately to be like the big kids, and even more desperately wanted her big sister to like her, took the glass and sipped. "Gee Tina, it tastes good! Just like lemonade, mmm! I like it. What's it called again?"

"Lemon gin."

"Gee whiz, imagine that. It's all together in one big bottle. You don't have to mix anything up, eh?"

Tina tucked her chin under and raised her eyebrows at Anna.

"Oh Anna, you're kind of square, aren't you? Mommy says its cause you pray so much with that old bat...How many times a day you gotta pray anyway?" She poured more gin into the second glass and handed it over.

Anna drank and replied. "Well, we go to church twice on Sunday, once in the morning, then for benediction in the evening. And we say the rosary every night after supper. It sure takes a long time. Harry didn't have to say it when he was with us cause he was so small, but Violette and me just about fall asleep. I don't think you should call Ama an old bat." Anna took another drink.

Tina started giggling. "You should hear what Mommy calls Ama besides an old bat! I wish you could stay with us instead of with Ama. We could have so much fun together. I could teach you lots of stuff, you know."

"Yeah?"

"Sure, about boys and things like that. I bet Ama doesn't even let you wear make-up to school huh?"

"Tin-AHH! Ama says make-up's only for fast girls who are looking for trouble! She says it's sooo bad and I'll go fry in hell if I even think of it!" Anna made a horrible face and sizzling movements with her fingers.

"Holy smoke! You're in grade eight, too, huh? I bet you've never even been kissed, huh?"

"Let's have another drink, okay, Tina?"

Tina poured up two big glasses. It was really easy to drink this time. Anna felt her nose beginning to go numb. She began giggling.

"So! You ever been on a date, little sis?"

"Are you joking? When Auntie Evelyn died last spring, cousin Linda had to stay with us for a few weeks until welfare could find her a foster home, eh? Linda's real pretty, just like you Tina, and she knows lots of kids. She even gets along with those real mean girls from the Willow Flats, Doreen and Mary Pauline and the one I really hate. Her name is Foo Foo."

"Foo Foo! What a dumb name!

"Yeah? You think so? But that's what they call her. She's got big fat cheeks like a chipmunk and little squinty blue eyes. Anyway, this big French family just moved on Latham Island last year. They took over the Rex Café. There's a girl and a boy about my age and they had another boy staying with them for the summer. He was from Edmonton. They all came to pick up Linda to go to the movies on Sunday afternoon. Ama said Linda could go only if she took me with her, eh? And Linda was giving me these real dirty looks and swearing about how I was a little goody-goody, but she had to take me anyways. Ama was watching out the window when they came and you should have seen her, Tina!" Anna got out of her chair to act it out. "She ran out of the house swinging the broom and started hitting all the boys on their backs while they were trying to run away. She was yelling at them, you devils, get away from my girls! The boys were laughing and Ama chased them at least two houses down the road."

"Holy Smokes! What happened then?"

"Oh, nothing much. Linda cried and cried, she was so embarrassed. We had to stay home. Linda was real happy to leave after that. I don't think she likes Ama too much now."

"So you missed your big chance to get kissed, huh?"

"I don't like kissing."

"How do you know if you never tried it? You didn't think you'd like the gin and just look at you now! You're on your way all right! Here, let's have a bit more."

"Holy moley Tina, won't Mommy know if we drink all the gin?"

"Nahh, don't worry about it! There's always more where this came from!" Tina poured out two more glasses. This time she filled them right up to the top.

"I've been so kissed!" Blurted Anna after she took another big slug from her glass, sloshing a bit on to the table. "You must promise not to tell, though, okay? I never told anybody before. It's too awful."

"Anna! You look like you're going to cry. Your not going to cry, are you? Here." And Tina scooted her chair closer so she could put an arm around her sister and pat her back.

"Tell me."

"The priest."

"Holy cow! The priest kissed you? Where was Ama?"

"She was sitting right there by the stove, where she always sits. I don't think she saw. It was this priest from somewhere else. He wasn't one of the ones here in Yellowknife all the time. He had a French name and he used to come and visit Ama all the time cause they would talk French together. And I always had to go sit on his lap and give him a kiss on the cheek, eh? But this one time, he put his mouth on top of mine and stuck his whole tongue right inside. It was so big and slimy Tina, I thought I was going to choke. I was trying to get away and he was holding my head in his hand so tight it really hurt. I was looking and looking at Ama, but she never said a word so as soon as he let me go, I just ran away. He doesn't come to visit very much anymore, but whenever I see him, I run away and hide. Sometimes Ama calls me to come and say hello to him, but I pretend I don't hear. I hate kissing! I hate priests!"

"Gee whiz." Tina hugged Anna. They drank the gin and looked out the window at the fleeing clouds before the blue. "Hey Anna, you okay now? You want to see something funny?"

"What?"

"I lied to you before. Mommy's not out, she's just in the next room. You want to see how grown-ups do it? Make babies? It's real funny!"

"She's in the next room? What's she doing? I don't want to see anything weird."

"Honest to Pete, don't be silly! It's real funny to watch! Come on." Tina stood up, taking Anna by the arm. Anna hung back. "But, who's in there with Mommy?"

"Doesn't matter. Come on, otherwise you'll never find out."

Tina pulled Anna in the direction of the second room. They tiptoed in, giggling and shushing each other. There was a blanket hanging on the window. The small room was very dark and very hot. Anna whispered loudly to her sister, "Too dark, Tina."

"Shh, I'll get a candle then, c'mon."

"Holy smoke! They'll see the light."

Tina began giggling again. "Nahh, they're too busy!"

The girls tiptoed back into the kitchen, got a candle and lit it from the big box of Blue bird wooden matches. Still giggling and hanging onto one another, they crept back into the bedroom and over to the bed in the corner. "Hold the candle closer Tina, I can't see nothing!"

"Shh!"

"But I can't see nothing at all, that guy's too fat, he's squashing mommy! He's covering her all up!"

Tina burst out laughing.

"*Holy shit! What the hell!*...Get out of here! Damn kids!"

Anna heard Mommy Suzanne's voice from underneath the man. She still couldn't see all of her. The man raised himself upon his arms to look at the two girls. Anna hardly noticed, she was staring at Mommy Suzanne. But Mommy kept her eyes closed and she turned her face to the wall. Anna felt upset, she hadn't seen her mother for a long time and now Mommy Suzanne wouldn't even look at her. What was wrong with her anyways? She stood there by the bed, unable to take her eyes from her mother, willing her to open her eyes and see that it was her, Anna, and not just any kid. Tina pulled her back into the kitchen. "Look at this, Anna! I got five bucks out of the guy's pants that were on the chair under the window! Let's go to the Rex Café and we can buy whatever you want."

The café wasn't very far away at all, it was still on Latham Island. Tina and Anna had a lot of fun. They played three songs on the jukebox with the bubbling pink and green lights. I love him, I love him, I love him and where he goes I'll follow, I'll follow, I'll follow. They ate french fries with gravy, salt, pepper, ketchup, and vinegar, and bought strawberry ice cream cones to eat on the way back. They scuffed along the sandy dirt road, watching the wispy clouds reflect the setting sun in the periwinkle blue sky. The last of the wild Alberta roses still bloomed here and there. Smoke from stovepipes drifted lazily towards the deep green lake. They reached the tiny house that Mommy Suzanne was renting that summer. Tina turned to Anna.

"I better go in first Anna, just to make sure Mommy's not too mad at us, okay? You wait here and I'll come tell you when it's all right."

Anna waited a long time. Finally, she knocked very softly. No one answered.

Anna went home to tell Ama about her nice visit with Tina and Mommy Suzanne. How clean the house was and everything was just fine and Mommy Suzanne had made them spaghetti and meatballs for dinner. With cake and peanut butter icing for dessert.

Leaving **HOME**

Mama Ama had cancer.

Ama clasped her hands together in front of her chest. "Oh what luck, my girls! To stay in the convent with the nuns. Oh, thank the good Lord. I don't have to worry about you now while I'm gone." Ama was taken away by the social worker in the car. Big blue fins at the back. It was snowing.

Anna and Violette were put in the convent. Sanctus. It smelled of paste wax and potato peels and long dusty black skirts.

"Ssst."

"Shush Violette. It's very holy here, eh?"

"I'm scared Anna."

"Sh, it's okay. Don't be silly. I'm kind of scared too, eh?"

The first night, Violette was taken away for a long time. She came back with her face all scrubbed shiny, in a new nightgown.

Anna was more grown up and she was sent to bathe by herself.

Anna flushed the toilet, she looked at the sink, and she washed her hands with the Dial soap. There were toilets and sinks at the school. There was no bathtub at the school. She looked around; she didn't know what to do.

She heard the swish of a nun's skirt, then a knock at the bathroom door.

"What is taking you so long in there? Run your bath, child."

There were two handles and only one place for the water to come out. She turned one handle. It made a lot of squealing noise; seemed like too much noise for the convent. She turned the tap off, her heart thumping. She turned it on again, just a bit this time. The bathroom became all steamy. Only hot water was coming out. Anna sweating. Oh quick turn it off. Turn the other handle. Now too cold. Now too hot. Anna panicked, whispering to herself. "Oh quick, turn it off. Don't play, you might break the bath tub. The nuns will be real mad. Please God, help me. I need to take a bath." Water was running down the walls. It was so hot. Anna tiptoed to the window and opened it. Anna took off her clothes and put one foot in the tub. She burnt her foot. Anna sat on the edge of the tub and cried. She was too bad to even take a bath when she was told to. She stood by the tub and rubbed little snatched handfuls of boiling hot water all over. She tried and tried until the water was cool enough to plunge her arm to the bottom. To pull the plug and drain the water. She dried and dressed herself in her pajamas. Opened the door to the frosty cool air in the hall and told the waiting nun that she was finished. The nun rustled by Anna.

She peered at the tub. "Don't you even know enough to clean the tub after yourself? You don't know what this is? It's cleaning powder for the bathtub of course. Don't act ignorant.

Why, you just sprinkle it on and clean the tub like this! Mon Dieu, the child doesn't know anything at all."

Oh God, this was really some place. She didn't know anything. Couldn't do anything the right way. The white way. They laughed at her for the way she ate.

"What are you doing? Hey, Look at Anna! Watch how she eats."

All the little girls around the lunch table put down their forks and stared. The white kids, the good kids, without the devil's blood, with white little fingernails. The kids who were never, ever afraid of faucets and telephones and things that plugged into the walls.

Anna was eating her meat by cutting it into long strips. She held one end of the long strip in her teeth and the other end in her hand. With the knife in her free hand, she cut off mouthfuls little bit by little bit. That way, she didn't need a fork.

It was Jolene DeCotret, the teacher's daughter. Again. "So that's how Indians eat meat, huh? Echhh, no one eats like that! Here. I'll show you. Leave it on your plate. *Now* pick up your knife and fork…hold them like this." Jolene smiled pretend-patiently at Anna. "Are you still following me? Tha-t's right. Now cut off just one little piece. That's right, now pick up the meat with your fork and eat it. Chew your food a hundred times with your mouth closed. For Pete's sake, why are you all red? Hey lookit her! She's blushing. Are you gonna cry *again*? Jeeez, I'm just tryin' to help you — Ga-aah, you're such a…a dummy! And stop making so much noise. Sister Agnes will hear and you'll get us in trouble. Jeez…" Jolene rolled her eyes daintily and looked at her best friend. Martha was Jolene's faithful shadow, so she rolled her eyes too and made a prissy little what-can-you-do mouth.

Anna stared at her plate. Swallowing big lumps of anger and roast beef and tears.

That night, Violette ate an orange in bed and hid the peels under her mattress and Anna was told they were filthy little savages. Anna beat her little sister up. Pinched her and pulled her hair and hit her because the nuns made her feel so bad. Then Anna had to go to early chapel and pray for her black devil soul all week. She was very angry.

Ama came back silent. Her face always ready to cry. She and Anna and Violette went back home. Ama spent all her time sitting on her red plastic chair by the stove. The house was very quiet.

It was bath time. They took the square tin washtub from where it hung on the big nail in the porch. They used the dipper to fill it with water from the big silver painted water barrel. They made a fire in the stove in the bedroom while the washtub heated up on the big stove in the kitchen. Then all three of them carried the tub into the bedroom and carefully, don't spill it now, placed it on a towel in front of the fire. Ama filled the big white enamel jug with cold water and added it to the tub so it was just right.

Violette bathed first, then Anna, and at the end, Ama. She sure had light skin, freckles all over. Her back like pale sausage meat. The kids would help her out of the tub, she always got stuck.

"*Hoy!* My little devils. Push-hh altogether *now!* Hup-ah-ha—*hup!*" They used soap to make her slippery.

Anna snuck a peek at where Ama's fat pink breasts used to be. Now there was only one. Now there was no place to pillow your head when you hurt. Shiny tight, pale and blue. Bony and purple and scary sad. To look away from.

Ama sat and smoked by the stove all day and all night. Anna

would fall asleep looking at the glowing little red fire from Ama's cigarette. She would wake up in a panic in the dark, not knowing where she was and feeling bit by bit until she got to the edge of the floating thing she was on. It was only after she went hand over hand all along each edge that she would remember where she was. Her bed at home. In the middle of nothing but dark. No walls, no door, no safety any more.

The next day, she and Violette asked Ama what it was like. The outside.

"See here is the hospital, my girls. The Charles Camsell Indian Hospital it's called. Nothing but Indian people in there, from all over the place. I took this photograph myself. With a camera. Pshawww! It was nothing I tell you. Easy. You just look in one end; there's a tiny little window, strong, like a blind man's glasses. *Then.* Click! It's just as easy as pie. Up top, you push a little button. After awhile, couple of days, maybe longer, hard to tell the time in that place, the nurse, she brings the picture. The photograph. Oh, it looks nice in the picture eh? But gee whiz. I sure don't like it there. Here. Get me my suitcase. I forgot, I made you something while I was in that place. To take my mind off my troubles you know." Poodles made out of cut up strips of a dry cleaning bag. A blue one for Anna, a pink one for Violette. "Ver-eee nice Ama. Ev-er good, eh Violette? Bee-yoo-tifull! Gee thanks Mama, Marsi cho!"

Pom-pom poodles with brown glass eyes.

It took Ama quite a few years to die after that first trip to the outside. The children were separated. Violette was put into the receiving home. Anna went to foster homes.

The social worker always said the same thing before each new and frightening door.

"These are very nice people, you'll like them a lot."

Two little boys. An orange telephone in the living room. Anna sat in her room. She looked all around. A bed, an empty dresser, her green duffel bag. She thought of Ama. "Be real quiet my girl, and don't get into mischief. You be good."

After a few weeks, the lady got real mad. "Why can't you sit around the table with the rest of the family like a normal little girl?" she said. So Anna sat at the table after dinner every night, until the lady and the man would look at each other and sigh, and tell her she could go. The lady was still mad. "You have to help out around here young lady," she said. So Anna waited in the kitchen, after she had sat at the table awhile. The little boys washed the dishes and she dried them carefully. Then she went to her room, so she wouldn't be in the way. The lady was still mad. "Oh, why can't you relate to us as a family?" she yelled at Anna. So Anna went down to the basement to watch the little boys play with their steam engine. She figured they might be easier to talk to. The steam engine was nice. It had round flat cakes of fuel. Sugary sparkling black. The little boys put the tiny pellets in the engine and lit them. Real steam came out. Shiny wheels went round and round; tiny arms pumped up and down. It was like the inside of an alarm clock. Only with whistles like the wind screaming in the fall. Anna liked the light from the tiny fire. It reminded her of home, sitting around the wood stove with the door open to see the flames, eating fish on the floor. And balls made of pounded dried meat with caribou fat, rolled in white sugar. Indian ice cream. Drinking tea with condensed milk made from contented cows. And listening to warm stories about devils and the Russians who were going to bomb the DEW Line. And the people down the road or across the town who had sold their souls to the devil to win at cards.

Often the foster family would go out to get a break. And Anna, who couldn't relate, would try over and over to throw herself down the basement stairs. When Anna had been happy in the bush at home, she had spent all days talking and singing to the things around her. Trees and roots and Violette and moss and clouds and water.

"Oh, that little girl," Ama would say happily. "Her head is in the clouds, I tell you, but I don't worry, let her be happy while she is a kid, who knows how it will be for her? At least she's smiling."

Now though, no more flying. Anna thought the people might like her better if she was hurt. She didn't know what to say to them. She tried falling off two steps, then three, and four. But it never worked. All the years of flying from rock to rock had taught her body to twist and land safely. Always.

"You'll like these people for sure," the social worker said.

You mean... maybe they'll like me, thought Anna.

This time Anna tried harder. She sat at the table and smiled and tried to look interested for at least ten minutes after each meal. She dried the dishes. She cleaned the tub. She always made her bed. She was quiet unless they spoke to her first, and then she tried to answer correctly.

Say please, say thank you, don't swear in dogrib...Disclenyeh! Don't talk ignorant.

Why are you so quiet? They asked.

Cat got your tongue?

I don't know what to say said Anna.

Just be yourself.

But myself is different from you.

Nonsense, Just relax.

I don't understand how it works here.

One time when they were out, she used up all the butter trying to make them cookies. She knelt by the stove and prayed, "Oh God, please make it work, I'll be real good, honest." But the cookies didn't work and in a panic, Anna threw everything into the neighbour's garbage can. Those Indians are so wasteful, don't you think? Of course they don't know any better, can't help it I guess.

Anna would try really hard to figure out how these people lived. When they were out, she went into their bedroom and looked at every single thing and put it all back carefully just exactly where it was before. But everything looked so clean and so new, as though it had never really belonged to anyone. The only time she made a mistake was when she chewed up one of the man's condoms, thinking it was some new type of gum. It was very hard to roll back up, and when she put it back into the box, it sure looked different than the others.

The social worker drove up to the door. By now, Anna had learned not to unpack her duffel bag.

"Well. You are causing us problems, Anna." Anna was scared. The cookies and the rubber thing. "But I just know you'll really like these people. And guess what? They are taking care of a little sister of yours! That's right! Suzanne's youngest; she's almost three. Shania! Isn't that lovely?"

And oh, but the social worker was wrong.

Anna knew right away. Right away from the pointed, sequined glasses on the pearl chain. So dainty. So lady like. Right away from the lady's rocket ship tits. Bosom, dear. *Nice* people call them bosom. The marshmallow blue banlon sweater set. The clean, clean kitchen. Right away from the locked up red knuckled scrubbed clean sanitized closed up tight smell. The meanest foster home.

This lady didn't fool around.

She made herself clear to Anna over lunch on the first day.

"Well, young Miss. Far be it for *me* to blow my own horn, but I sacrifice, do you hear? I truly do sacrifice myself for kids like you. Now I know, there are people in this town...*I'm* not the type to name names...But there are people who take unwanted children for the cash, or the glory. But they don't understand the Indian children, they try to be nice to them, baby them too much. Yes. Well I know that it's all pure baloney. Yes indeed, just out and out baloney. You listen to me and I can teach you how to be just as good as any white person. I can teach any half breed or full blood how to do well for themselves. All you kids really need is a strong hand in the right place; do I make myself clear? You just need plenty of good food and a *lot* of watching. Oh, I'm on my toes with you little buggers, there's no mistaking that."

The lady's husband worked all day. He was to be called Father. He called her Mother. The lady said he took up too much room and was too dirty from work, so he had his own room at night.

Father had to change his clothes and have a bath before dinner every night. Then he went to his room and went to bed. Oh the things she did for him. That man would be such a mess if it weren't for her, why, she even cut his toenails. Men were so helpless, she told Anna.

Shania and the other foster child, a little boy who looked to be about a year older, were very quiet. They never smiled, had lots of naps and baths, and looked scared. Anna had to watch them play, it was good training for her in later years if she made sure that they didn't get dirty, or make messes or loud noises.

Anna gave up on trying to figure out white people, and spent her time hiding. But the foster mother had very sharp eyes, and she was always somewhere, behind a wall or around the corner. She knew when Anna threw her lunch in the garbage. "Why half the town, and I don't think I need point out *which* half, would go down on their *knees*, yes, on their knees, if they could eat this well. Just imagine, throwing a perfectly good salmon sandwich out! Arrogant, yes, that's what it is. You need to learn respect and humility young Miss, you certainly do."

Half the town. The roast caribou head. So tender and the tongue and sweet cheeks saved for the children and the oldest grannies. The half-smoked trout spitting and bubbling on the grill over the fire. The crisp crackle between the honeycomb of the beaver tail, and sometimes, in the spring, a fat young muskrat. Ptarmigan and roast moose head and boiled bear meat. Hot bannock with enough salty butter melted on it to run warmly down your chin. Piled high cranberries simmered in just the right amount of sugar. The smoked and dried caribou meat with its white pink lace of fat to melt silky on your tongue. And now and then, oh what luck, some nice fat fish eggs to put in the bannock.

Then the lady caught Anna drawing dirty pictures of fully-clothed women with giant bee-hive hairdos and swollen coned tits and high heels. With their bums sticking out and wearing earrings. And fishnet stockings. Every day Anna was caught at something she didn't even know was wrong.

"Tell me, what *were* you doing in there? What exactly is it that you do in your bed at night, so that every morning, the sheets are half on the floor and the pillow all filthy damp? The social worker told me about all your sneaky little ways. I know what your kind is like. Don't you worry about that! And you think I don't know? I saw you yesterday. Letting the younger children play in the mud with my kitchen spoons, teaching them how to be just as filthy and irresponsible as yourself.

"Oh, I saw you all laughing together. Well, they're too young to know better. I just wonder how you were raised, filthy savages! You listen to me. *Decent* folk do not use their kitchen utensils in the mud and the dirt. Dogs poop out there, and not even nice little pet dogs, sled dogs, for Pete's sake! How will I cook now? Now that my flipper is covered in dog poop? *Tell me that!*"

The last day, she found a pack of matches in Anna's wet jeans pocket. "Oh my heavens! And to think I trusted *you* to go out for the afternoon unsupervised. Who did you sneak off to meet? And at your age, too. Who gives you cigarettes when you sneak off into the bushes like you do? Ignorant, ignorant girl. You'll wind up in trouble soon enough the way you're going! Go to your room, I can't bear the sight of you."

Anna and her friend Rose. Walking on the endless, ageless rocks with the sky so low and silvery grey. Clear pine smell. The smoky blue berries like blind raven eyes in the spiky green bushes. Finding hollow and sweet reeds tender in the rich moss and smoking them, pretending to be grown up ladies. Holding hands, talking and talking. Laughing.

The social worker came. Her lips were tight.

The new foster parents had no children. The lady liked fat paperbacks with lots of catastrophe and ladies who married rich cruel men at the end. When they were out Anna took baths with little bits of the lady's Avon bubble bath. She drank little bits of the man's scotch. Tried on all of their clothes, even the lady's bright red pantaloons with lace at the knee. She examined all their photographs and read all their letters. Read all the bills and cookbooks. The man was a teacher at Anna's school. He taught English. And the lady was the school secretary. They wanted Anna to be bright.

"Why there was a fellow at university, native, but bright as a whip, wasn't he dear?" The man looked at the sweet, always-there smile of his wife, cleared his throat. Harrumph. And went on.

"Had to work twice, three times as hard as most of the other fellows, and came from a poor background naturally. Never did hear what happened to him later on. But there's an example for you Ann. You plug away at the books, and who knows where you'll end up! Why, you might even become a secretary like the Missus here."

It was January. Mid-term exams for grade nine. Anna leaping through the moonlit field behind the house. Barefoot in the snow. Drinking sneaked coffee and using aspirin and guilt to stay awake. Setting the alarm for five a.m. to study again. In between the memorization, she ran and leapt t-shirted through the snow banks. Wishing for pneumonia. Not to have to write the exams. They wouldn't like her if they found out that she was nothing but a dumb Indian. The next morning, she went in to make pancakes for them when they returned from church.

The lady gushed. "Oooooh, how *did* you get all those little holes in the middle? Isn't that just so clever? Chris, come look at this! Indian pancakes! Did your mother teach you? How fascinating!"

"Uhhh no...it's your Aunt Jemima mix."

Anna stayed with them twice. She thought they liked her, but.

The social worker returned. She drove Anna across town to a new home.

"We're taking you because no one else will have you. You know that, don't you? You really think you are a hard case, don't you? Well don't you worry, the whole town knows of your reputation by now…It's not pretty, believe me…no. Not-at-all."

Her file listed Anna as being sullen, apathetic, unresponsive, and antisocial. Please, my girl, you be quiet and polite. Just stay out of the way…don't make no trouble. Withdrawn. Isn't that a different way of doing it. Is that an old Indian custom my dear? Fuck off, I'm trying to do it your way. Sneaky, dishonest. Walking on the rocks, making cookies and throwing out the batter, throwing lunches in the garbage, looking at the foster family's things…trying to figure them out. With hostile tendencies…Wipe that smirk off your face. *Why* won't you just try? We are only trying to help. Just look at yourself young lady; look at the advantage you have over most of your kind. In the mirror, brown hair, brown eyes, white skin. Why no one need ever know that you're part Indian. And she was fourteen. She began to drink. What the hell was so wrong with being herself? Why did the world make such a big deal about White or Indian? She just felt like a person. A plain old ordinary person.

"Yes, we know which direction you're headed in…Just like all the rest…boy crazy and booze crazy. We've tried and tried. Why, I've told you all about myself for one thing. Tried to tell you how a proper lady should act. Why, I've even taken the time to show you how to do a proper manicure. I do not really know what else a decent person could do for you. And we are your last chance, young lady. I hope you have brains enough to realize that much."

Anna shared a room with the baby. She had searched this

house from top to bottom. Since she was headed for boys and booze anyway, Anna took the flashlight from the tool kit in the basement and the books from the top bedroom shelf. About ladies and engines. Anna laughed and laughed. In the same room as the baby too. And when the thin, white-faced foster mother confronted her. What do you think anyways, that I read your sex books aloud to the baby every night? Maybe we share a mickey while we're having a good laugh together, eh?

And Anna had a pet, a mouse she saved from the family cat. She talked to it late at night. The lady found it and confronted Anna when she came home on her lunch break. "And keeping that filthy beast in with the baby clothes! Her tiny white diapers and the hand-knitted sweaters covered in mouse droppings."

The foster mother's face had gone from white to purple. Only her nose stayed white around the edges. Anna stared.

"Get rid of that mouse at once young lady. And I don't have to tell you what you can do with yourself afterwards, do I? *Well* do I?"

The woman looked as though she would explode any minute, or go wheezing off crazily around the room. A filled up balloon let go to lose all it's air. She let out a warning whoosh. "*Pack your bags.*"

Anna took the mouse to school. Cats scratched her legs and howled. She ran and ran with all the hissing behind her. After school there was no one in the house but Anna. She ate all the aspirin in the medicine cabinet. At dinner she threw up and packed her bags.

And Anna went to another home. The native foster children had their own cubby holes in the dark, wood-panelled basement and could do as they pleased.

And Ama came home for a little while. Anna and Violette went home. They were strangers. Anna was in grade ten and Violette was in grade five. The high school was across town from the elementary.

Ama went back to the hospital. And Anna went to another home. And Ama came home for a little while. The children returned home. Ama went to the hospital again. And Anna went to another home.

Ama died. Anna ran away from her foster home.

She worked a split shift in one of the gold mines. She was fourteen. Every night she got drunk. She stayed away from men though. When she closed her eyes, she saw Ama. "Oh, my girl, don't wind up like your mother please. The devil's blood. You were born with liquor in your blood…I never told you but now you're old enough. Your mother, she was drinking all the time she was carrying you and you were born with that booze in your blood. Born drunk. You just about died. Be careful you don't turn out like Suzanne. Men and drink. My poor girl, Suzanne. It was those men that turned her to drink, and now they keep her there. She has no love in her life. Those men just use her and throw her away like an old rag. That's what they do to Indian girls. That between your legs, my girl, it doesn't belong to you eh? It belongs to God. It is Jesus' little chalice. And those white men, you don't believe a word they say all they want from you is one thing. You know that, eh? Oh, they'll talk so pretty, but when they get what they want, they'll leave you in the ditch…just like they did to Suzanne."

So for Anna, no men, she was afraid of them. She resented them, feared them, their so easily assumed power. She stayed out of their way. That fall, Anna quit her job at the mine and began to work as a waitress in the Yellowknife hotel. The social worker found her there in mid-September and took her to another foster home. She was fifteen now, but still not of legal age. Anna began grade twelve. She was numb.

High HOPES

Anna woke in the hospital.
What was it, dear?
Wake-up pills. There was a little red rooster on the box.
How many?
Dunno...couple boxes maybe

Then the tube scraping up her nose and down her throat, gagging her. The charcoal wet sour liquid burning back up. Then long muffled weeks alone on the high bed in the small square white room.

She found her clothes in a closet at the end of a long hospital hallway with shiny brown linoleum floors. She put them on and left. Ran through a side door, through the waist high snowdrifts to the main road. She went to see the social worker with the hooded eyes.

When she left the welfare office there were two policemen waiting.

The car so hot but snow no melts. Fast...quiet. Canoe through the reeds whhh-shhhhht. Honey-coloured wooden paddle melt-slicing through the green ice cream lake. The dinosaur hiding waves.

Back to the hospital. White nurse guards now. Blue guards before.

R.C.M.P.

If you don't watch out, that big policeman, he'll take you away.

Be Nice.

How?
Please just tell me.
What's nice?

White is nice. White guards. White jacket. White straps. There's a no-colour pain in her arm. White sleep snowdrift. Then, dreaming dark in an airplane. Warm in an airplane. Can't move. Must be sick. All tied up in an airplane, dreaming of Ama before she died. "When you grow up my girl you get out of this place you hear me? People will say I'm wrong, but you never mind. I'm thinking of you. Your skin is so white no one will give you any trouble. You get an education for yourself, it doesn't matter how. You get out of here. Promise me now before I go."

Tied down with straps, flying under a hospital blanket that smells like a drowned uncle.

The plane landed at night. There were so many lights. Anna

was outside. Wicked, unknown Edmonton. Ice cold air on her face. Ambulances made her feel excited.

More guards.

Who do you think you are with all those fancy words? Just because your skin is so white. Yer nothin' but a god damn crazy squaw. We know it and so do you, don'cha you bitch. Fucking stuck up bitch.

Heavy ring of keys in the nurses pale hand. Locked doors. Barriers, steel mesh, long tunnels with night-light, rows of beds. Funny smell of dog food. They unbuckled the strait-jacket. Take a bath now dear. Put on a nightgown. "Why is this one here? She looks okay to me."

Anna couldn't be nice. She wasn't really white. She just looked that way. Where was she? Where is this place?

She thought, I don't know why I'm here I don't know where I am I don't know where I was supposed to go. Am I sick? Do I have T.B.? What's the name of this place?

Oliver. Ponoka. Edmonton.

Oh boy, she made it to the outside. Anna was in Edmonton. Was everyone there crazy?

 Yeah.

Wow.

I'm not crazy. I'm Italian and I have cancer of the breasts.

The Italian woman left. She was married to the baker in Yellowknife. Boy oh boy, they made nice long johns there. So fat and spongy, donutty with crispy soft white icing, and they had a juke box with neon pink and turquoise blue lights swirling about. Anyone with a dime could listen to Blue Moon with twinkling Christmas lights all around even in August.

Anna's crying.

Barred windows. Chain nets across the glass. Rustlings from the rows of bed lumps. Soft gold gleam of night light on the linoleum. Floating dull into grey sleep.

Blue moon

You saw me standing alone.

Without a dream in my heart.

In the morning in the mental place. In the morning in the nuthouse. In the morning in the loony bin.

Get dressed dear.

It's healthy for you to meet the others.

I'm not nuts. My stepdad says I'm just spoiled. I'm not nuts. I'm a runaway. I'm not nuts. I'm twelve, I'm going to have a baby too. I'm sad. I'm nuts. I'm upset. Let's throw our bananas at the clock. Me nuts? They say I'm too young to be a working girl, like they know anything about it. I told Joe not to go out into the field, Joe...don't go. I'm just an old whore at heart. I carried a cross from Banff to Calgary on Good Friday. Hey kid, you know what a dyke is? I'm just here on holiday and if you could see my old man you'd know what I mean. I hate. I steal. I love you.

Not now dear. Later...when doctor comes.

How do you feel when you see some one spit on the street?

On this ward you have a choice. Some sign in, some sign out. Only, like if you're a kid, then you got no choice. You can't sign out. But you can choose to come in if you're under-age. You know, like if you don't want to go to jail. That's why most of us are here. Some choice eh? Here or jail. Yeah. And if no one wants to take care of you, then you wind up here too.

Bastards.

Shock? What's shock?

Oh baby cakes, you don't wanna know.

Where do you keep your pills?

Under my tongue, in my hair, in the toilet, I save mine for bath time. I'll save mine for you if you want. Wanta trade?

Little chickenshit.

Anna went for walks. To be tested. Long underground tunnels with brown linoleum floors.

She saw

laundry rooms. White. Blood. Steam. Shit. Javex. Puke. Clotheslines. Steel beds with giant rubber wheels and canvas straps. Padded rooms behind small steel meshed windows. Only a mat on the floor. Old people dribbling and one died. Anna had to feed them. Red and bony. She curled their not-really-there hair. They peed their clothing, the bedding, the towels, the wheelchairs, the strait-jackets. Anna saw pale green curtains pulled round the dead beds. She saw soup pots big as tanks. Lost bodies knocked out with dope. People sitting in plastic orange chairs in dim yellow halls, crying. With no noise. The optometrist. Operating rooms. Big blinding lights green like spiders. Then tied to freezing narrow steel, ice wires taped to her head. Smell of rubbing alcohol. People shells. Then she woke up back in her bed in the rows and rows of others.

Anna saw. Her file.

She asked the other girls.

What's a manic-depressive? Such a fancy name.

What'cha do to wind up here anyway? You say you're part Indian huh? Hard to believe. You sure don't look it. But that explains a lot huh?

You're wrong. I bet a manic-depressive is something real weird. Maybe I really am strange. Maybe like I just never knew it, just never really knew I was nuts.

Oh Christ, don't be stupid. They call you manic-depressive or schizoid or whatever, it don't mean nothing. What happened just before you came here?

My Ama, my mom died.

Then what?

I dunno, the welfare kept putting me in white foster homes, one after the other. I was upset but no one would listen to me. They'd just tell me I was bad and a lot of trouble. Then I'd go to a new foster home.

They just wanted to get rid of you, that's all. They like to keep you Indians in jails and loony bins. Teach you your place, you know? Keep you out of trouble. Get you out of their hair.

Ohhh is that why? Maybe they like to keep us drunk, too. I heard that the government up north pays for some of the cost to ship booze up. But it doesn't pay for food to be shipped up. Who the hell are *they?*

What gives them the right to be? They?

I'm going to find out.

No one listened to Anna. Was that weird? No one listened because she was a half-breed kid.

But Anna was going to get out of Ponoka by the spring. She knew it.

And when she did,

the whole wide wonderful world would be there.

Just waiting for her.

She knew it.

DENENDEH

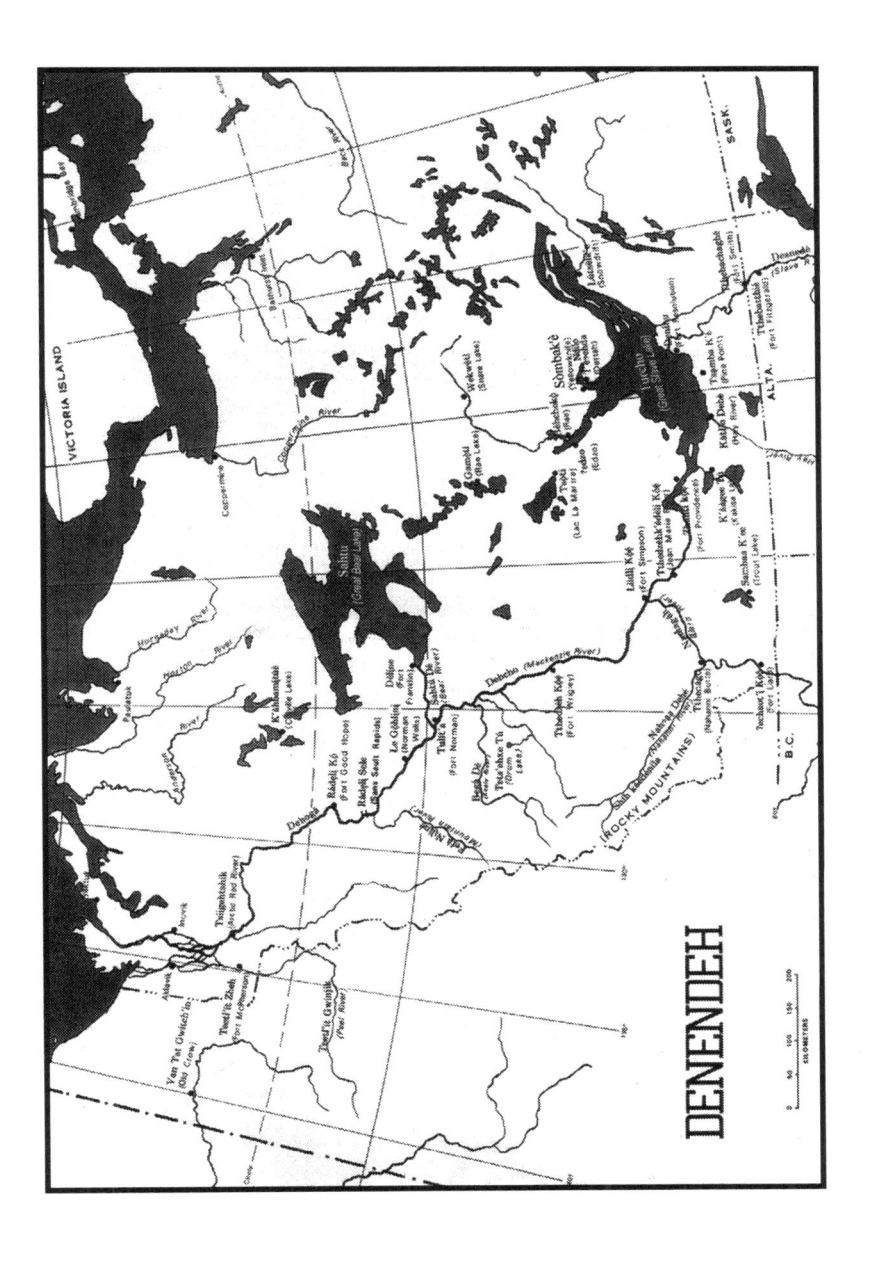

FRANCES BEAULIEU has been developing the stories in *Little Buffalo River* since graduating from the Ontario College of Art in 1982. She is Métis, born in the Dene Nation, Denendeh, and adopted as a baby by a woman from the Denesóliné (Chipewayan) family. She lived in Sòmbak'è (Yellowknife, Northwest Territories) until she was sixteen and now lives in Toronto. She is a writer and family historian who works as a food columnist for the *Toronto Star* and a security guard at the Royal Ontario Museum. She is blessed with a large and loving family. *Little Buffalo River* is her first book.